SPORT

SPORT

Louise Fitzhugh

A Yearling Book

Published by
Dell Publishing
a division of
The Bantam Doubleday Dell Publishing Group, Inc.
666 Fifth Avenue
New York, New York 10103

The trademark Yearling® is registered in the U.S. Patent
and Trademark Office.

ISBN: 0-440-48221-6

Reprinted by arrangement with Delacorte Press
Printed in the United States of America

February 1982

10

CW

BOOK ONE

Chapter 1

"Don't you understand that I was once fifteen years old? That I looked at my mother the same way you're looking at me? That I see the hatred in your eyes and the despair and the love and all of it?"

"I'm eleven," said Sport. "I'll be twelve next month."

Charlotte Vane had turned away. Her long, thin body leaned toward the window, her forehead touched the drape for one brief second, and then she turned back again.

"You've got a goddamned literal mind. You listen to me, little boy, because you've got one or two things you better get into your head right now. I'm not a dreamer like your father. I like money. I like money very much."

Sport sat looking up at his mother, his face blank. He shifted one leg uneasily.

"And don't wiggle. If there's anything I hate more than little boys, it's wiggling little boys."

Sport had a dark feeling, like being an unfriendly spider. I want to get out of this room, he thought, I want to get out and go back home and make my father pick up his socks.

"Your grandfather, Simon Vane, the old wretch, is down there in that sitting room dying right this minute. Your grandfather liked money a lot. Your grandfather made thirty million dollars. Made it. Do you understand that? He made it himself. He got up in the morning and he went downtown and he made it."

Sport thought of the thin, small body downstairs, of the hands you could see through, the gaunt, tiny head, the clouded, unseeing eyes, eyes that used to light up, and the mouth that used to say, "Ah! Here's my boy! Here's my real son," whenever Sport walked into the room.

"He didn't sit around all day in front of a stupid toy, tap-tapping, tap-tapping, that damned tapping, you couldn't get away from it. He didn't dream . . . *dream* about writing a book. Where did a book ever get anybody?"

Sport opened his mouth and then closed it. He had wanted to say, "But he published the book. Dad published the book and it was good. He gets royalties. I know just how much." But there wasn't any use. What were those royalty checks next to thirty million dollars? The figure loomed in Sport's mind. He saw himself writing it in his ledger, the one where he kept track of the household spending for himself and his father. He saw it written in red ink. Imagine *owing* thirty million dollars.

"I know what's in your dirty little boy's brain," said Charlotte loudly. Sport jumped. "I know you want to get away from me. I know you wish to God I'd go back to wherever I came from and never come back. You want to crawl back to that dirty hole of an apartment your father lives in, where he can't even buy you a pair of shoes, much less enough to eat." Charlotte turned and screamed, "He's *no good*. He's a rotten, *no-good bum*, your father!"

Sport held his breath. He felt somehow that this was the dead end of his mother's rage. She couldn't go any further. There was no further to go. He waited, watching her gasp, start, and then stop herself from continuing and turn away.

With her back turned to him, she said quietly, "Get out. Get out of this house."

Sport got up quickly. He went out the door and closed it quietly behind him. Once in the dark hall, all his breath came out in a long whoosh. He stood a minute listening, looking into the gloom of the big old house, then ran as fast as he could down the steps.

Chapter 2

As Sport put the key in the door to his apartment, he heard a loud groan from his father. He looked toward the kitchen and saw immediately that his father had, as usual, boiled the coffee left over from breakfast.

"I just can't get the hang of it," said Mr. Rocque sadly.

"There isn't any hang to it, just watch it so it doesn't boil," said Sport.

"I know," said his father. "I just start working and forget it's there." He started to go back into his study then, remembering, he looked at Sport. "How did it go?"

"Okay," said Sport, going into the kitchen. Mr. Rocque came after him. Sport tried to busy himself by looking in the icebox, but there was nothing in the icebox to look at.

"How was your mother?" said Mr. Rocque finally.

"Okay," said Sport.

"How's the old man?"

"Dying."

"Well put. Did you see him?"

"Yes."

There was a silence. Mr. Rocque went over and sat down at the kitchen table. "It isn't pretty, death." His voice was quiet.

"No," said Sport.

"I wasn't sure you should go over there at all," said Mr. Rocque. "Your mother insisted." He sighed and looked out the window. "She has certain custody rights, you know. Since she's out of the country so much, she feels that whenever she comes back, she can get you over there."

Get me over there to yell at me, thought Sport.

"When the old man dies, your mother will be a rich woman." Mr. Rocque looked searchingly at Sport.

Thirty million, thought Sport.

"Is your mother still beautiful?" asked Mr. Rocque.

Like a witch, thought Sport. He climbed on the stool and got some peanut butter down from the shelf.

"I suppose she is," said Mr. Rocque, not expecting an answer.

"She's ugly," said Sport. "Ugly and mean."

Mr. Rocque's mouth dropped open. "Was she nasty to you?"

Sport looked at him. If I tell him what happened, he thought, he'll get mad and call her up, then she'll get mad and then they'll both end up yelling and then everybody will be yelling.

"She's just mean. I *see* she's mean."

"She is that. But did she say anything to you?"

"She said that Grandpa was dying, and that he had thirty million bucks, and that he worked for it every day." Nobody can make anything of that, thought Sport with satisfaction. It's all true.

"Thirty million! Whew!" Mr. Rocque gave a long whistle of astonishment. "No wonder that old geezer fought so hard to get you. Imagine leaving all that loot to her. She'll juice it down the drain of every gambling table in Europe."

"Fought to get me?" Sport looked at his father.

Mr. Rocque looked at Sport. "You're old enough to talk about it. He tried to get your custody away from me or your mother. He wanted to raise you himself. He used all the power he had, which is considerable. But the court couldn't see turning you over to an old man in a big empty house, no matter how much money he had. Your mother was, of course, unfit."

Unfit, thought Sport.

"I guess you wonder what unfit means," said Mr. Rocque. "It means to the court that having you would have been the same to her as having a trained poodle. You would have been left in every hotel room in Europe and the Far East. I don't think she has any more notion of how to raise a child than Lawrence of Arabia. So you got stuck with me." Mr. Rocque grinned and Sport grinned back. "Not that I'm much better at it. Sometimes I think you're raising me."

Sport laughed. His mouth was full of peanut butter sandwich, so it wasn't easy.

"Drink some milk, son," said Mr. Rocque. "Get strong and grow up and support your old man."

Sport laughed some more. He felt at home. All of those old decisions about his life had been made when he was four years old. It was all a long time ago and he had had no part in it. Of his life before living with his father he remembered only a white sunny room and a white starched nurse. He had had visits with his mother every time she was in town, but they had been strange, impersonal trips to Brooks Brothers to be outfitted, then lunch at a restaurant. He hadn't even been able to eat because his mother had given him so many directions about table manners that he had become frozen, had finally sat, stiff and starving, while she ranted about the terrible ways he was learning from his father. None of it had ever made any sense. He was always watching the time, waiting until he could get out of the long black car, run up the steps and into the cheerful mess that meant home.

"Speaking of money," said his father, "do we have any?"

Sport stopped chewing and looked at his father.

"I know, I know," said Mr. Rocque, "but I don't need much."

Sport calculated quickly in his head.

The last royalty check, which had come in April, was gone. Another wouldn't be here until next month, October, and there was no telling what that would be. The checks for him which came erratically from his mother were not to be depended upon. The checks which had come regularly from his grandfather had stopped abruptly with his illness. Sport's ledger showed that after the seventy-five dollars they paid for rent had been deducted, they would have thirty-two dollars and eight cents.

"What do you want it for?"

"I've been seeing a girl . . ."

"Oh, no."

"Now don't get excited, Sport. This one doesn't like expensive things. I just want enough to take her to a movie."

"Is she coming here?"

"Yeah, for a drink, at six."

"A drink . . . *of what?*"

"Don't we have anything?"

"No, and we can't buy any."

"A beer then."

"One beer," said Sport.

"You drive a hard bargain."

Sport clenched his teeth. One beer and that was it.

"What about dinner?" he asked his father.

"Well, I thought I'd take us all to the Olde Heidelberg. That knockwurst and sauerkraut is great and doesn't cost much. She doesn't care, honest, Sport. She's a nice girl."

Sport looked at his father closely. His father looked out the window, a trace of embarrassment on his face.

Nice girl, nice girl. How often have I heard that, Sport thought. I've yet to see one who could live on our income. In fact, why didn't any of them take us to dinner? If a man *obviously* didn't have any money, wouldn't you think it would occur to them? But no . . .

"Okay," he said finally. "That means forty cents for the quart of beer. Three dollars each, at least, at the restaurant. That makes six dollars. I'll stay home. There's a can of soup. Then two-fifty each for the movie . . .

"Can't you take her on a walk through Carl Shurz Park?"

"Look, I'll tell you what . . ." Mr. Rocque began.

"Do you realize you're already up to eleven

dollars and forty cents and you haven't even tipped the waitress?"

"I was going to say, let's wait and see. Maybe she won't want to go to the movies."

"Fat chance. I never saw one that didn't." Sport started washing his milk glass.

"This one's different. Let's wait . . ." Mr. Rocque smiled. "You'll see." He got up and started for his study.

"Do you want any lunch?" asked Sport.

"No," said Mr. Rocque and was gone.

"Are you working on the article?" yelled Sport.

"No. The novel." The door to the study slammed and there was silence.

For the article, thought Sport, he could get two thousand dollars and for the novel he may get nothing. So he works on the novel. Figures. Sport smiled to himself. It was still better than living with that witch.

He decided to go over and visit his friend Seymour.

Chapter 3

Seymour lived over the candy store his mother ran. He often helped behind the counter. Sometimes his mother let Sport help too while she went into the back to have coffee and rest her feet.

Sport ducked around the corner to York Avenue. He passed the stationery store where he bought his father's typing paper and waved to old Mr. Crane who ran it. He passed Melnikoff's where old Mr. Melnikoff always asked if anyone wanted a shopping bag. He turned into O'Neil's candy store.

"Hey, creep," said Seymour as he entered.

"Hey, creep," said Sport.

"Hi, Sport," said Mrs. O'Neil.

"Hi," said Sport. He hung around not knowing what to do. There was only a young boy in work clothes drinking coffee at the counter.

"Take your coat off, Sport, you'll catch your

death," said Mrs. O'Neil. "Hang it up in the back there. Then come give us a hand."

There was a table and four straight chairs in the back, and a cot for Mrs. O'Neil to lie down on. Sport hung his coat up and went back into the store.

"What can I do?" he asked Mrs. O'Neil.

"Feel like scrubbing?"

"Sure," said Sport.

"Have a go at this sink, then," said Mrs. O'Neil.

Sport pushed up his sleeves and went to work. It was pleasant. Mrs. O'Neil laughed and joked with the men who came in to get coffee. Most of them were workmen from the big apartment house that was being built nearby.

"The sink's clean," said Sport to Mrs. O'Neil.

Seymour had filled the Coke machine. "Here," he said to Sport, and pushed across the counter a sparkling, ice-filled glass of Coke.

"I got some time off now," said Seymour. "Wanta go upstairs?"

"Okay," said Sport.

"Be back here by five," said Mrs. O'Neil. "The rush starts."

"Okay," said Seymour. They started out. Just as they got to the door, Seymour grabbed a whole pile of comic books.

"Hey, you!" yelled Mrs. O'Neil.

"I'll bring 'em back," yelled Seymour as they ran out the door.

They ducked into the hall and up the steps to the O'Neils' second-floor apartment.

"Whatcha get?" asked Sport.

"Everything. I piled 'em up this morning when it was raining. It's one each of all the new ones. Only keep 'em clean. They gotta go back on the rack."

"Great," said Sport, and flung himself down in a chair.

"You like Bims?" asked Seymour from the kitchen.

"What's that?" asked Sport.

"New kind of candy bar. Man sold it to my mother but nobody buys them. I'm hooked on 'em." Seymour came back into the room with a pile of candy bars. "Here, try one."

"Hey, Seymour," said Sport, his mouth full of candy.

"Yoomph?" Seymour had put two candy bars in his mouth at once.

"I saw my blanking mother today. She yelled her blanking head off at me." Whenever Sport or Seymour were very upset about something, they used the worst language they could think of. It made it better somehow. When things got beyond the pale, they used blanks because nothing was bad enough to express it.

"You got a mother?" asked Seymour.

"Yeah. You know. The one took me to that blanking Brooks Brothers for the blanking suits."

"Oh, yeah. I'd punch her right in the mouth." Seymour was forever punching everybody in the mouth. He chewed pensively. "Thought she blanked around Europe all the time."

"Did. Back now."

"How long?"

"My blanking grandfather's blanking out altogether." Sport felt a twinge as he said this. He rather liked his grandfather. Seymour's eyes looked wild with curiosity. Seymour was fascinated by anything to do with death. His mother kidded him and said he would grow up to be a mortician if he didn't watch out.

"Yeah? What's he got?"

"Old age."

"Neat," said Seymour. "That's for me."

"Yeah," said Sport. "I'm planning to live to ninety-six."

"I'm immortal," said Seymour, eating happily.

There was a noise at the window. Seymour jumped up and looked out. "It's Harry," he yelled and opened the window. "Hey, creep, come on up." He leaned so far out, Sport thought he would disappear.

"Guess his blanking mother's off on a blank. I

could punch her right in the mouth," Seymour said as he went through the room to the front door.

Harry burst into the room. He was tall and thin, a chocolate color with shining eyes.

"Hi, Sport, how are you, man?" He flopped down in a chair.

"Hey," said Sport.

"Hey, got any more?" Harry asked Seymour, pointing to the candy.

"Yeah," said Seymour, and going to the kitchen, he got four candy bars for Harry. They watched him eat in silence for a minute. He ate with great concentration, as though he were doing a math problem with his teeth.

After two candy bars he joined the world again. "My blanking mother," he said slowly, "had better watch her blanking self or I'm going to blank the blank out of her."

"What she do?" asked Seymour.

"Got so blanking drunk that she fell out the window."

"Yeah?" Sport and Seymour yelled together.

"Blanked right out the blanking window." Harry was enjoying his audience.

"You mean right out onto York Avenue?" asked Seymour.

Harry nodded. "Splat," he said.

"Did she break anything?"

"Are you kidding? Take more than that for my ol' lady. Bounced like a ball, she did." Harry's accent got very British. In the last year he had taken to English clothes and ways. Today he was wearing a tight suit, the jacket buttoned all the way up over a turtleneck sweater, and high boots.

"Hey, man, they're good those things you got there," said Seymour, suddenly noticing.

"Gear, what? Yeah . . ." said Harry, drawing out his breath in a long sigh as he looked down and admired his clothes. "But I tell you. I think something should be done about women."

"Like what?" said Seymour, eating again.

"Like . . . well, you could start by getting rid of them." Harry pursed his lips and looked up at the ceiling.

"Wonder what it would be like?" said Seymour, a grin coming over his face. "With no women at all."

"Yeah," shouted Sport. "That's good. The League for Extermination of Women." He turned it around in his mouth.

Harry looked around and picked up a piece of paper. He wrote something. "If we make it League for the Extermination of Women Dangerous to Small Boys, the initials spell L-E-W-D with an S-B on the end!"

"Hey, great," yelled Sport.

"We could have uniforms," shouted Seymour.

"Yeah," cried Harry. "Maybe with red hats."

"Like the Black Muslims," yelled Sport.

"Don't laugh, man," said Harry, suddenly serious. "Not funny."

"Hey"—Seymour was laughing—"you a Muslim, Harry?"

"I am for *me*," said Harry. "I am with nobody." He looked suddenly thinner in his dark suit, thin and hard as a post stuck in the ground. "Think anybody gonna care about you?" he asked suddenly, pointing a long finger at each in turn. "*You*. That's who gonna care about you." He said this so quietly, meanly, confidently, that a silence fell as he ended.

"Not my blanking mother, anyway," said Sport finally.

"There you go," said Harry, pointing at Sport. "Now you got the mush out your mouth." He seemed to lose interest then, and walked over to the table to pick up a comic book. "Hey." He turned back to Sport. "I didn't think you even had one."

"I do. She just doesn't live with me."

"Yeah?" Harry seemed interested.

"She's a beaut," said Sport.

"What she do?" Harry flopped into the chair. "Fall out of windows?"

"No, but I think she'd like to throw me through one." Sport saw himself sailing through the air past Brooks Brothers, all dressed up.

"That's what my blanking mother was just about to do," said Harry, pausing dramatically.

"What?" said Seymour. He and Sport looked at him.

"She ran at me," said Harry, nodding his head. "She ran at me to push me out the window and I ducked. I just slid down on the floor and she went flying past me."

"Wow!" said Seymour.

"Geez!" said Sport.

They stared at Harry in admiration.

Suddenly Seymour jumped up. "Hey, it's getting late," he said. "We gotta help in the store. You wanta come, Harry?"

Harry roused himself from the chair. "Naw. I gotta go on down the hospital." He went past them and out the door without looking at either of them.

"See ya, Harry," said Sport.

"Yeah," said Seymour to Harry's back. "To-morrow, hey?"

"Yeah, man," said Harry and disappeared.

Seymour locked the door and they ran down the steps. "Come on. Mom'll kill me." Seymour ran so fast, Sport had to jump three steps at a time to keep up.

They ran into the candy store.

"'Bout time," yelled Mrs. O'Neil above the noise of the line of jabbering, laughing men jammed against the counter. "Two Stooges I got working for me. Get back here. Here. You, Sport, make the toast, put out the butter, mayonnaise. Seymour, get on the grill."

"Grilled Seymour," muttered Sport.

"Coming up," yelled Seymour, and they dove into work.

Chapter 4

At five thirty Sport knocked on the study door.

"What?" came the muffled response.

"It's five thirty and if she's coming at six, you better get dressed."

"Okay," said Mr. Rocque. Sport could hear the electric typewriter go off, then some rummaging around and the door opened. His father looked red-eyed, exhausted, and about as far away as China. He looked down at Sport, smiled vaguely, and rumpled his hair. "Get a clean shirt on yourself." He smiled ingratiatingly. "And let's have a good time, son. You worry too much. Let's go have a good dinner and go to the movies."

Sport looked at his father. His father did work hard. He knew that. It wasn't his fault that all that working didn't make much money. "Okay," he said and smiled.

His father stumbled into the shower. Sport went

to his room and got out a clean shirt. He had already washed his neck and ears.

"That you, Kate?" yelled his father.

Kate must be her name. He hesitated a minute, hoping his father would hurry, then realized he wouldn't and went to the door. She was standing right there when he opened it. "Hi," she said and smiled. He liked her voice. She was tall and thin, with blond hair. Her eyes were wide and blue. She didn't look like she had so much money as to be dangerous, although her clothes were good.

"Think I could come in?" she asked softly. Sport turned red and, opening the door wide, he let her in.

"Is your father here?" she asked.

"Yeah," said Sport. "Uh, sit down. He'll be out in a minute."

She took off her coat and put it on the back of a chair. Sport grabbed it and hung it up.

"Oh, Dad's getting dressed. Can I get you a drink?"

"No, thanks, I'll wait. This is a nice apartment," she said, looking around.

She must be bats, thought Sport. Figures. When he gets a nice one, she's crazy.

"Well," said Sport. He shrugged. Then he felt like a fool for shrugging, so he turned abruptly and went into the kitchen. He got a Coke out of the icebox and came back, trying to look non-chalant. His feet felt ten feet long. He sat down across from her and drank the Coke.

She didn't say anything, and in one way he was glad of that. He looked her up and down, then concentrated on her shoes. He had long ago discovered that women who never intended to marry had very sharp, very pointed, very delicate and special shoes as though they spent every bit of money they had on shoes and far be it from any baby to need anything that would deplete the shoe money. Women who could or could not marry, depending upon how they felt, had ordinary shoes. Kate's shoes were just shoes.

"Is there a snake under the couch or are my shoes on fire?" Sport almost dropped his Coke. Caught staring, he grinned. She laughed. At that moment the door opened and Mr. Rocque stepped out of his room.

"Ah, Kate," he said, and striding across the room, he leaned over and kissed her cheek. Sport looked him over. He had on his best flannels, a red sweater, a striped shirt, and no tie. Good, he thought, the Olde Heidelberg.

"Well, well," said Mr. Rocque, "what'll you have, Kate?"

No, no, thought Sport, not what'll you have, but will you have a beer.

"What have you got?" asked Kate.

Good girl, thought Sport.

"Well . . . there's some nice cold beer," said Mr. Rocque, giving Sport a crucified look. Sport looked away stoically.

"Sounds lovely," said Kate.

"Good," said Mr. Rocque and whipped into the kitchen.

Sport sat looking at his sneakers. There were sounds of glasses, bottle openers, and the muffled mutterings that always emanated from Mr. Rocque when he did anything. Sport couldn't look up. He knew he looked silly sitting there staring at his feet, but he was caught in a vise of shyness.

Mr. Rocque appeared finally with two glasses of beer.

"Here," he said triumphantly.

Kate smiled and took a sip. "Cheers," she said.

"Cheers," said Mr. Rocque, and then they looked at each other.

Uh-oh, thought Sport.

The telephone rang. Sport jumped up and answered it.

"Hello."

"Hello, who is this?"

Sport hated that. "Who is this?" he asked sharply.

"This is Miss Carruthers, Mr. Vane's secretary. Is Mr. Rocque there?"

Sport knew Miss Carruthers. She had a large mole on her forehead with six hairs in it.

"Yes," he said. He turned to his father. "It's for you, Dad."

"Oh?" said his father and came to the phone.

"Hello. Yes. Yes, Miss Carruthers. Oh. Oh, that's too bad. Oh, I see. Well . . . I don't know. Well, he's a little young for that sort of . . . I understand that. This sounds rather like an order, Miss Carruthers, a royal command. . . . I'm not being flip. I just can't see that it would do any good. What? Not particularly. All right, put her on."

There was a long pause. Mr. Rocque turned and gave an exasperated look at Sport (who was now watching him). "It's your grandfather . . ." he began, and then to the phone: "Oh, hello, Charlotte." There was another long pause.

"Now, Charlotte, take it easy. Don't scream. Let's think of this thing in as mature a way as possible . . . Will you stop screaming? . . . Now, look here, ol' girl . . . well, you're not *young*. . . . Besides, pleasing you and playing up to the old . . . Well, just tell me what good it will do . . . you will *not* come and get him. . . . Oh, for God's sake, Charlotte, all right, I'll bring him." And he hung up on her.

He turned back to the room looking as though he couldn't remember where he was. He stood silent for a minute looking at them both.

"Get your coat on, son," he said briefly. Sport stood up. "I don't know what to do about the evening, Kate. His grandfather is dying and his mother thinks he should be there. The old man has asked for him."

"Don't be silly, Matthew. I couldn't understand more." She stood up. "We'll have other evenings." She smiled sympathetically, and Mr. Rocque's face went from gloom to a sweet glow the way a smoldering fire will suddenly light itself.

"I just have to drop him off. They don't want me around there. Then I'll take you home."

Sport stopped in the doorway to his room. "You gonna leave me there?"

"They want you to spend the night, son."

"What for?" asked Sport, horror breaking over his face.

"The old man . . . well, he may go before morning."

Sport looked at his father. He felt a kind of panic. "What am I supposed to do about it?"

"That isn't it . . ." began his father.

"I can't stop him," said Sport, fear rising now in his throat. What do they want me for? he thought. What am I supposed to do?

"I know it isn't any of my business," said Kate, "but it does seem a bit much."

Thank you, lady, thought Sport. He looked at his father, who looked uncertain.

"I'll call her back," said Mr. Rocque, and went to the phone. Kate sat down again. She looked at Sport. Sport looked away.

"Let me speak to Mrs. Rocque—Miss Vane, I mean," said Mr. Rocque.

He sounds nervous, thought Sport. Don't you fink on me, Dad. Don't do it. Not about this.

"Charlotte. I'll bring him over to see Mr. Vane, but he won't spend the night." Mr. Rocque sounded quite strong and definite. There was a long pause. "No. That's definite. I'll bring him over and then come back for him in an hour." Another pause. "If it gets worse, I'll stay there with him."

Yeah, Dad, yeah, thought Sport.

"Sorry, Charlotte, that's it." And he hung up again. He turned around and looked at Sport. Then he smiled. "Just get a sweater and your jacket. We'll go on over." He turned to Kate. "If you don't mind, maybe we'll just go have a beer and wait for him."

"Good," said Kate. "That sounds better." And she smiled at Sport.

Sport was too nervous to smile back. He went into his room. Have two beers, have a Scotch, anything, just don't leave me in that house. He grabbed his jacket, put on a turtleneck sweater and his windbreaker over it. There was a hole in the sweater. Maybe she won't see it, he thought, maybe she won't start screaming.

He went out into the living room just as Mr. Rocque was kissing Kate's forehead. He started to turn back into his room but his father said, "Let's go, son, and get it over with."

His father and Kate had their coats on so they all went out the door and down the steps.

"Where's the car?" asked Sport.

"Here, just in front," said Mr. Rocque.

"Wow, you got lucky."

Mr. Rocque opened the door of their small two-seater. "Here, Kate, let Sport get in back. There's just room enough for him." Sport climbed in. He always felt good in the back. It felt snug, like a ship's cabin. When he sat in front he pretended he was driving a racing car, which wasn't hard, considering the way Mr. Rocque drove. He laughed to himself. Kate was about to get her first demonstration of the world's worst driving.

They were off to a racing start. Mr. Rocque had forgotten that the car was still in gear, so when he started the engine, they leaped forward like a horse rearing.

"Ride 'em, cowboy," said Kate.

She has a sense of humor, thought Sport, which is good because she'll need it.

They swerved away from the car parked in front and did sixty down York Avenue.

"He's not dying right this minute, is he?" called Kate over the roar of the motor.

"No," yelled Mr. Rocque.

"Then could we slow down?" screamed Kate. Sport giggled.

"Sure," said Mr. Rocque, slowing down so suddenly that there was a blare from a taxi behind. "Uh," he said wonderingly, "that too fast for you?"

"No," said Kate, "I always breathe this way, in gasps."

Mr. Rocque now went twenty miles an hour. Sport started to chew his nails. "My, look at the scenery," said Kate. They went two blocks and she couldn't stand it any more. "Okay, okay, you win, but how about trying those numbers there in the middle? Like thirty and forty?" She looked at Mr. Rocque.

"They've never been used," said Sport. "They probably don't work."

Kate gave a whoop of laughter and turned and looked at Sport with real appreciation. She almost broke her neck for her trouble because Mr. Rocque was off and flying again.

"Navigator to Bombardier," she yelled to Sport, speaking into an invisible microphone. "Watch your tail. I think the front part's gone."

Sport started to laugh and couldn't stop.

"You know what it is?" said Kate confidentially. "It's a machine, and he doesn't believe in them."

Sport was still laughing. He began to like Kate

a lot. All the other girls had either screamed in terror or pretended to love the way he drove, which had only made him worse.

"It's as ridiculous to him as a coffee percolator," said Kate, looking at Mr. Rocque as though he were a guinea pig in a laboratory, "and he drives it like one, I might add."

Mr. Rocque said not a word, but spun around corners, dove into side streets, hurtled across avenues as though he were a grumpy bus driver.

"Here we are," he said triumphantly, screeching up in front of a fire hydrant.

"The tires!" said Kate. There was a terrible noise and Sport laughed.

"What?" said Mr. Rocque.

"Nothing," said Kate. "I lost my head for a minute."

She turned to look at Sport. "Courage," she said sweetly.

"Just think, no matter what you go through, it won't be half as bad as what I'll be going through just trying to get a beer."

Sport laughed and was out of the car before he remembered to feel bad. Kate pulled his head down and kissed the top of it.

"We'll be back," she whispered in his ear.

His father unfolded himself from the car, straightened his jacket, and took Sport by the hand up the steps of his grandfather's brownstone. Sport looked back once and Kate waved. She's nice, he thought, she really *is* nice.

Mr. Rocque stood in front of the door. "Don't do anything you don't want to, Sport. Don't let them push you around." He looked into his son's eyes a minute, then pushed the buzzer. "I'll be back in an hour," he said.

Chapter 5

A man in a white coat opened the door. Mr. Rocque nodded and said, "Hello, Howard, take good care of him."

"Yes, Mr. Rocque," said Howard. Sport walked in after getting a little push from his father.

"See you in an hour," said Mr. Rocque and went down the steps.

The door closed. Howard helped Sport take his jacket off. It came as a shock to Sport to realize that his father knew all the servants, that of course he would, because he had lived there, had been married to that witch. Married. Sport shook the thought out of his mind.

"Are you hungry?" asked Howard in a kind way.

"No, thank you," said Sport. He stood very still, hoping no one would see the hole in his sweater.

"Here's your mother now," said Howard, and went away with Sport's coat.

"Darling," said Charlotte. "Darling, come here

to your mother." She stood in the library door. He realized with a great deal of surprise that she had been crying. Why is it suddenly darling? he thought. Is there someone else in the library to hear her?

He went to her. She smothered him to her, and he felt a wave of revulsion. What is this? he thought. I don't even know her. She pulled him into the library and then he saw. There was a tall, older man standing by the fireplace.

"This is Mr. Wilton, darling, your grandfather's lawyer."

"How do you do," said Sport. He shook hands, then grabbed for the hole in his sweater. It was on his left elbow so he held his right hand over it.

"Sit down, Simon. Would you like something to eat? Or a Coke?"

"No, thank you," said Sport. How can you drink a Coke holding your elbow?

"Have you had dinner?" asked his mother in a bored way as she sat down.

"Yes," Sport said, because he knew that if he told the truth, she would make him eat.

"My, your father eats early," said Charlotte, and looked at the lawyer and laughed in a snide way.

"*He* hasn't eaten," said Sport. And then, because he knew it would make her angry, "They're out to eat now."

"They?" said Charlotte and gave her worst witch look.

"He and Kate."

"*Kate?*" said Charlotte in such a way as to say, Who in the world would be named Kate?

It had backfired. What do I say now? thought Sport. I never should have started this. I should know by now never to open my mouth around her.

"Who is Kate?" she asked, serious now, angry.

"A friend of my father's," said Sport in as manly a way as possible. There, he thought, what can she say to that?

"Have they been friends a long time?" she asked in a silky voice.

"Ah . . ." Mr. Wilton began, "Charlotte, do you think we should ask the nurse if we can take him in now?" He cast a sympathetic glance at Sport. "Your father is picking you up in an hour, I understand?"

"Yes, sir," said Sport gratefully.

"Oh, well, in that case," said Charlotte, apparently in a fury. She flounced out of the chair and left the room. As the doors closed, Sport realized with horror that he was sitting alone with Mr. Wilton. What shall I say? he thought hurriedly. There was little time to be worried because Mr. Wilton started immediately.

"There are a couple of things I would like to

ask you before your mother comes back. First of all, do you get along all right with your father?"

"Yes, sir," said Sport softly.

"Just all right, or is it all okay there?"

"It's . . . all okay there." What funny words, thought Sport.

"Good. Then you have no . . . there have never been any regrets that it didn't work out differently?"

"*No, sir,*" said Sport with such vehemence that Mr. Wilton smiled, then laughed.

Sport laughed too then. I don't know what I'm laughing about, he thought, but he seems all right, this guy.

"I haven't seen you since you were four years old."

There was never anything to say to this, so Sport said nothing.

"You seem to be growing up quite sensibly." Mr. Wilton turned and looked at the small fire in the fireplace. When he turned back, he seemed to have arranged his thoughts. "Does your father make enough money?" The words came out like a machine gun and Sport answered before he could think.

"No, sir," he said, then, watching Mr. Wilton's face, he added, "I mean, we have enough to live on."

"You're not in need?"

I don't know what that means, thought Sport. Does he mean do we need money? Because we do. Maybe he'll give us some.

"Don't you know what I mean?"

"No, sir."

"Then you're not in need."

"Yes, sir," said Sport, thinking, He's not going to give us any money. He looked around the rich room, the creamy pattern of the carpet, the thin legs of chairs, the rich quiet held in by the heavy draperies.

"You have a hole in your sweater though."

Sport jumped and grabbed his elbow.

"No need to be embarrassed. It's not your fault."

At that moment the doors opened, and Sport's mother came back.

"He's very weak," she said to Mr. Wilton, "but they think he should see him now." She looked at Sport. "He's been asking for you." And then she turned her head away fast as though she were crying. Mr. Wilton moved toward her and put an arm around her.

I don't believe her, thought Sport. She doesn't mean it, she's pretending.

"I'll take him in," said Mr. Wilton.

"No, I will," said Charlotte quickly, and again there was the rage.

I don't get it, thought Sport, it's like she's planning something.

"Come on," she said harshly and stuck out a thin hand to grab him. Sport, for some reason, looked at Mr. Wilton. Mr. Wilton nodded. He got up then, took his mother's hand, and allowed himself to be led to the door.

They went down the hall, and then into a large room very much like the library, a room with the same heavy quiet about it. At one end of this room, however, a four-poster bed had been set up, obviously from upstairs. A starched nurse rose from the chair as they came in. There was a figure on the bed. It didn't move at all. Maybe he's dead, thought Sport, and nobody knows it.

His mother led him to the bed. The nurse's face went all crinkly and she tried to smile.

"Well, now, and there he is, the little darling, and we'll be so glad to see him, won't we, there?" She leaned over and screamed at the thin yellow head. Her voice seemed more a voice in a cheap bar than a sickroom.

There was no response from the head. "There, now," she said even more loudly. "Been asking for him, you have"—she poked the pillow viciously, "now you don't even look at him."

Sport wanted to run quickly and grab his grandfather in a fierce hug. He wanted to jump in between the old man and this evil woman, give the yellow head a kiss on the withered cheek, yell, "Good-bye, Gramps," and run from the room. Once in the air, he would cry, run all the way home, and forget the whole thing. That would be good, not messy and strange like these two screaming, pretending women.

The old man stirred. A weak sound came out of his mouth. The nurse took Sport's hand and pulled him roughly to the side of the bed. She did it mechanically, as though she had done the same at a thousand deaths, as though all families were inadequate to see to their deaths.

Sport stood close to the bed now, could see how clean and starched the sheets were, could see into the open cavernous mouth. His *teeth* weren't in there! That's what it was! Sport realized suddenly that he had never seen anyone without teeth. He began to feel funny—hot, and then clammy and cold.

A long breath came out of the mouth. "There, now," bellowed the nurse. "It's your own boy to see you. He's here, come to see you."

A long breath, then another, then so softly as almost not to be heard, "Si-mon?"

"Yes, and it is," yelled the nurse, "your own Simon."

"Simon," said the soft breath with satisfaction. The eyelids flickered, tried to open, became still again, the mouth closed. From the coverlet came a thin, hawklike, yellow hand that traveled crablike toward Sport.

"Take his hand, that's a good boy," cried the nurse as loudly as though they were all on the other side of a river.

Sport grabbed the hand quickly, because he knew that if he thought about it he wouldn't be able to do it, like taking a spoonful of medicine. The hand did not feel like a hand, but only like a bunch of thin, brittle sticks, too small to make a fire with. The hand was aware of his with only the weakest of pressure. Sport squeezed the hand softly and suddenly there was strength, suddenly the hand held his in a grip he wouldn't have thought the old man capable of, and it wouldn't let go. Sport pulled his hand a little, and the grip tightened. He turned around and looked at his mother to know what to do. As he did so, he caught a curious look on his mother's face. She was staring at her father with more hatred than he had ever seen on a face.

The breath came again. "Si-mon. My son. My Simon. My boy. My only boy." The hand relaxed as though the exertion of these few words were finally too much.

The nurse leaned over and pulled back Sport's hand. Then she put her hands on his shoulders. "There now, seen you he has, and very good it is too that he's recognized you. Very good. Doesn't it please you, son?" She turned him around with her fat, hard hands and looked at his face.

"Come on," said Charlotte. She took his hand as though it were a dirty handkerchief. Again the rage, the hatred, seemed to flood her face. She seemed unable to control it.

I wonder if an hour is up, thought Sport, as they started toward the library. Halfway down the hall, his mother turned him around, put her hand under his chin, made him look at her.

"What did he want in there?" she asked. He looked at her stupidly. "Wilton. What did he ask you?" She wanted to know badly. He could smell how much she wanted to know.

"Nothing," he said.

"Tell me, you little jerk." She yanked his arm as though it were a leash.

"Nothing," he said calmly.

She led him along the hall then, back into the library. As she opened the door, he almost shouted with relief because his father was standing there.

"I came back early," said Mr. Rocque. "I'm just not too sure about this whole business."

"Oh," said Charlotte, "how's Kate?" She dropped Sport's hand, went over to the sideboard, and poured herself a drink.

"What?" said Mr. Rocque.

Sport went and stood by his father. Out of the corner of his eye he could feel Mr. Wilton watching him. I wish I had told Dad to wear a tie, he thought. He looked at Charlotte. She had been talking for some time, and he just tuned in on the end of it.

". . . so it looks like you're in for a windfall, Matthew. And from the looks of you, it's about time." She twisted her thin body into a chair.

"What is she talking about? Do you know?" Mr. Rocque turned to Mr. Wilton.

Mr. Wilton moved urbanely across to the bar. "I'm afraid I'm not at liberty to talk about this." He fixed a drink in the silence that followed and then looked at Charlotte. "We all may be in for a few surprises, my dear. I wouldn't jump before the horse does."

Sport saw Charlotte hurtling a fence. He wanted to giggle. He wanted to run home and wash his mind out with soap.

"Come on, Sport," said Mr. Rocque and turned Sport around with one hand. "I never did know what your mother was talking about."

"That's for sure," said Charlotte. Sport stood with his back to her. He didn't want to look at her ever again. He heard his father walk across to Mr. Wilton.

"Good-bye, James. Nice to have seen you again."

"Good-bye, Matthew. You have a good little son there."

"Thank you." Sport could hear the pride in his father's voice.

"Simon." His mother's voice hit the back of his

neck like a razor blade. "Come here and say good-bye to your mother."

"Good-bye, Charlotte," said Mr. Rocque, and walking swiftly to Sport, he opened the great doors and pushed Sport out into the hall.

"God. He'll never change," came Charlotte's voice as the doors closed.

Mr. Rocque stood a minute, his face tight. Looking at him, Sport thought, He wants to go back in there and smash her. If he does it, I'll help him.

"Where's your jacket, son? Ah, here . . ." Mr. Rocque said as Howard came around the corner holding the jacket like a dishrag.

He helped Sport into it and then nodded to Mr. Rocque. "When it happens, Howard . . ." said Mr. Rocque, "I wish you would call me first."

"I will, sir," said Howard, then with the faintest of bows he showed them to the door.

Once out into the air Sport looked around wildly for the car and, he realized with surprise, for Kate. The car was parked in front of a garage door with the largest sign Sport had ever seen saying emphatically NO PARKING. He ran to it, pulled open the door, and clambered into the backseat.

"Hi there," said Kate. She smiled her wide smile. "Bet that was a barrel of laughs."

"You know it," said Sport.

"Hungry?"

"Starving." He laughed from sheer freedom.

"Well, there's this here old German-type restaurant . . ." said Kate, ". . . where I hear they got
some knockwurst and sauerkraut. . . ." She winked
at Sport. ". . . and there'll still be enough left over
for the movie!"

Sport's mouth fell open. "It's no good, son," said
Mr. Rocque. "She's part of the family already." He
looked at Kate with a simpering smile.

"What's the movie?" asked Sport.

Mr. Rocque started the car. It bucked a few
times and then roared down the street.

"I don't know," yelled Kate, "but let's hope it's
not a drive-in. We'll go right through the screen."

Chapter 6

The next morning Sport woke up to find that it was raining. Without getting out of bed, he turned his head and looked out the window. There was a mist from the direction of the river, and a branch from the backyard tree of life flapped mournfully against the pane. He watched the drops roll slowly. He thought, Gramps is dead.

Why did I think that? he asked himself sharply and looked up at the cracked ceiling. Maybe he is dying this very minute, and I'm the only one who knows it.

When will I die? Not until you are old, he remembered his father telling him, not until you are old and wise and very happy. He thought of himself dead, in a short casket because he was eleven, with only his father leaning over him and crying. The thought of his father crying was more horrible than the thought of his own death.

He got up, reached for his socks, and thought

of his mother. His mother would be out of town for his funeral. It's a wonder she wasn't out of town for my birth, he thought with irritation; it's a wonder she didn't phone it in. Ever so much nicer, my dear, and so much more sanitary. He could hear her now.

The phone rang in the living room. He jumped up, then heard his father padding across the floor to get it. He stood still, holding his breath, listening.

"Yes?" said Mr. Rocque, then after a long pause, "Ah." Probably the publisher, thought Sport, and reached for his other sock.

"I hadn't intended to bring him there every day," said Mr. Rocque. Sport stopped dressing and listened again.

"*I* don't even know Aunt Carrie, Charlotte, why should he for heaven's sakes?"

Oh, no, thought Sport, not again.

"All right, all right, but for God's sake have them all there at once. I can't keep dragging him over there. . . . I *know* he's your child. Since he's your child why don't you think about what all this mess will do to him? Oh, rubbish . . ." Mr. Rocque slammed the phone down. Sport could hear him padding out to the kitchen, clattering around, starting to put the coffee on.

Sport pulled on his jeans, an old sweater, and,

leaning over, tied his sneakers. I want to go ride my bike, he thought petulantly, or play ball with Seymour.

"What's happening?" he asked as he came into the kitchen. His father looked up out of his early morning fog.

"Oh . . ." he began and turned the coffee down . . . "your mother wants you to come over to the house and meet her sister."

"What for?"

"I haven't the faintest idea."

"Rats," said Sport and sat down at the table.

"Rats, indeed," said his father. "I think," he said, putting some bread in the toaster, "that we'll just forget the whole thing."

"Yeah?" said Sport, with a wide grin on his face.

"Yeah," said his father and looked at Sport with a warm smile.

"Hey, great. I'm going out and play ball maybe."

"It's raining," said his father absently, taking two burned pieces of toast out of the oven. "Well, I blew it," he said, looking at the toast. He picked up the two pieces and started toward the garbage can.

"No. Wait," said Sport. "We can save those." He grabbed the two pieces, took a knife, and scraped off the burned part into the sink. He put each piece on a plate and showed his father.

"Good boy," said his father. They started to eat. The phone rang again.

"Oh, no," said Sport.

Mr. Rocque got up and answered it. "Listen here, Charlotte. Do you expect to call me every fifteen minutes?"

You'd think they were still married, thought Sport. You'd think she still owned him.

"I don't give a knockwurst what time you want him there, because he's not coming."

Sport laughed and put some jam on his toast. The kitchen felt warm and cozy with the rain outside. He looked through the red-and-white checkered curtains, sewed haphazardly by an old girl friend of his father's by the name of Mitzi something-or-other. A willow wept against the panes.

". . . and if you think I am any kind of guy that would make my son even walk across the street to get one cent, then it didn't do you a bit of good to be married to me."

I haven't been listening, thought Sport. What money? What's he talking about?

"Forget it, Charlotte. He's got better things to do with his day." There was a pause. "He doesn't *stand* on street corners. What kind of a woman are you?"

Stand on street corners? Sport thought of the older guys on the block, standing on the corner, showing off new clothes, making jokes, yelling at girls. When I'm older, he thought, I'll do that, me and Seymour and Harry.

His father yelled then, an outraged yell, the yell he usually reserved for his agent. "I've *had* it, Charlotte!" He banged the phone down so hard, Sport thought he had broken it.

Mr. Rocque was so mad that it took him a minute to cool down. He appeared finally in the kitchen, sat down, and drank some coffee. "There's something going on," he said finally, almost to himself, as though there were no one in the room. "She's got some sort of plan that needs . . ." He remembered Sport and locked up. "I don't get it, son. She wants you over there more than is reasonable. You can't *help* any. There's nothing for you to do there. I don't get it." He drank some coffee. "What happened when you were there? Did Mr. Wilton say anything to you?"

"He asked me if we had enough money."

"And?"

"I said yes."

Mr. Rocque smiled. "Anything else?"

Sport hesitated. "He said I had a hole in my sweater."

"Did you?"

"Yes."

Mr. Rocque was no longer listening. He looked toward the window and moved his lips around.

Moving his lips around was a sign to Sport that some intense thinking was going on. He waited, hoping he would be let in on the answer when it came.

"I think . . ." said Mr. Rocque, and then stopped.

"What?" Sport couldn't help himself.

"No. I don't know. I don't know enough about money and wills to figure it out. But I do know that if it didn't have *something* to do with money, your mother wouldn't care if you were in Alaska. It's something to do with money, the old man, and you, but I don't know what."

Thirty million, thought Sport, but it was too big a sum to think realistically about. It sounded like something the government would spend to send up a missile.

"Can I still go out?" he said finally.

Mr. Rocque looked at him. "Sure," he said. "Stay as long as you like."

Sport jumped up. "Are you gonna be here for dinner?" he asked his father.

"Oh, I forgot to tell you. Kate's going to come and cook for us," said Mr. Rocque, all smiles.

"When's she coming?" he asked his father.

"'Bout six," said Mr. Rocque. "You like her, son?"

"Yeah!" said Sport.

"Well," said Mr. Rocque, rubbing his clipped head with embarrassment.

"So long, Dad," said Sport.

"So long," said Mr. Rocque.

Sport jumped down the stairs. One flight down he saw the landlord coming in the front door. Sport turned and ran back into the apartment.

"Hey, Dad, I forget to tell you. Write the rent check. Mr. Collins is right downstairs. You could give it to him and save the stamp."

"Okay, son," said Mr. Rocque, smiling.

Harry lived over on Eighty-second between York Avenue and First Avenue. Sport went up the steps to his apartment. The building was the same kind of building as Sport's. The halls smelled of cabbage and cat pee.

He knocked on Harry's door.

"Yes?" came a girl's voice from inside.

"It's me, Helen . . . Sport."

Harry's sister, Helen, opened the door. She was very pretty, somewhat lighter in color than Harry, and about the same size even though she was seventeen. She went to Hunter College, and typed manuscripts for a living.

"Hi, Helen. Is Harry here?"

"Sure, Sport. How're you?"

"Okay." He came into the living room. There wasn't much furniture, only a couch, two armchairs, and a card table that Helen had set up by the window to do her studying on. There wasn't any rug, nor any coffee table.

"He's back in the boys' room," said Helen.

Sport went on back along a small hallway, past one bedroom with a big double bed into another bedroom with another big double bed.

In the middle of the bed, his long black boots propped against the headboard, lay Harry, reading a book.

"Hey, Harry," said Sport.

"Hey, man." Harry swung his long legs around and sat on the side of the bed. He grinned. "What's up?"

"Let's go play ball," said Sport.

Despite the rain, they played all afternoon. At about five thirty they went home.

Coming up the steps to his apartment, Sport heard angry voices. He stopped outside the door. His father said, "That's ridiculous. Just because I don't know where he is doesn't mean he's *up* to anything. He's eleven years old, not four. He has friends in the neighborhood, they play ball, things like that."

"I can imagine what friends," said Charlotte.

Sport realized with a shock that his mother was in the apartment. To his knowledge his mother had never been in the apartment. He began to itch. It wasn't right her being there. It was like getting out of a shower and running into Winston Churchill.

Sport moved away from the door. I'll go out and wait'll they leave, he thought, and turned to go, but his father's voice said: "I take care of him!" He sounded desperate.

"He could be dead on a street corner for all you know," said Charlotte.

I have to go in, Sport said to himself. The poor guy's really getting it.

He opened the door.

His father turned around. His face flooded with relief. He didn't say anything.

"There he is," whined a sharp voice, and Sport looked over at a woman he'd never seen before, sitting beside his mother on the couch.

"Hello there," said his mother. "What have you been up to?" She was smoking a cigarette in a long holder and had a martini in front of her. She must have brought her own gin, thought Sport.

"Hi, son," said Mr. Rocque. Sport looked at him and nodded and then looked at the strange woman. She was older than his mother, but she looked like her. She looks, Sport thought suddenly, the way my mother is going to look. She was all sharp lines, baggy-eyed, tight-lipped, long-legged. Her eyes were small and mean. Her hands, folded across her lap, were long, with long yellow fingers. Looking at her, Sport felt unaccountably afraid.

"This is your Aunt Carrie, Sport," said his father.

"How do you do, Simon," said Aunt Carrie rather primly, as though she were making a point about his name.

"Tell us what you were doing," said his mother insistently. She took out a flask covered in paisley and filled her glass.

"Are you hungry, son?" asked his father. Sport nodded, not taking his eyes off the women. They held a horrible fascination for him, like two crows on a fence.

"There's some cake, take a glass of milk," said his father.

Sport went into the kitchen. As he got out the cake and milk he could hear them talking.

"Won't that spoil his dinner?" asked Aunt Carrie.

"He's not big on manners, is he?" said Charlotte.

He heard his father sit down in the armchair with the broken spring. "First of all, it won't spoil his dinner. Have you ever tried to spoil an eleven-year-old boy's dinner? They don't spoil. Second, his manners are fine."

"Well," whined Aunt Carrie. "I must not have heard him say hello."

Sport winced.

Charlotte lowered her voice so much that he had to strain to hear. "Aren't you even going to *ask* him where he was?"

"Of course not," said his father loudly. "I trust my son."

"Well," sang Aunt Carrie.

From the *slinck* made by the broken spring Sport could tell that Mr. Rocque had stood up. "It's been very nice meeting you, Carrie," he said, rather wildly.

"Is this a dismissal, Matthew?" began Charlotte. "I have my rights, you know."

"Charlotte!"

Oh, fizz, thought Sport, he's lost his temper.

"Don't start, Matthew. You might as well control yourself. We have a whole lifetime together."

"We precisely do *not* have a lifetime together."

"I mean a lifetime of making decisions about Simon."

"I make the decisions," yelled Mr. Rocque. "And the first one is that you get out of here."

"Well, my heavens," said Carrie.

"Come along, Carrie. He always was a boor."

"I never heard of such a thing," said Carrie.

"Don't think about it, dear," Charlotte said in a silvery voice as they went down the steps. "We don't, thank God, run into many people like him. Just dismiss him. He's about as important as a bad martini."

"Oh, my," said Carrie, and they were gone.

Sport went to the kitchen door. His father was standing at the hall door. His back looked bent and tired. He turned around and saw Sport. For a moment it seemed as though he didn't know how to look and then he laughed, saying, "How do you like that for a couple of cats?"

Sport laughed.

"Hey," said his father, coming into the kitchen, "how about that Carrie for an old bag?"

"Who's she?"

"Your mother's older sister. And not that much older either."

"What did they want?"

"Purportedly for you to meet Aunt Carrie, although why this should be considered such a delicious project I can't imagine. It shows something, though. The clan is gathering. They're up to something. I wish I could find out what it is."

"Why don't you ask Mr. Wilton?"

Mr. Rocque looked at his son with surprise. "Not a half-bad idea. I'd have to think how to phrase it though. Nothing has really been done or said yet. It's just a feeling I have."

"Wonder what Kate will cook for dinner?" said Sport, trying to get his father back into the room. He hated seeing his father involved with his mother in any way at all.

"What?" Mr. Rocque looked at him blankly.

"Dad!" Sport looked exasperated.

"What? Oh, sorry, son, I was thinking. What did you say?"

By now it seemed inane.

"I just wondered what Kate was going to make for dinner."

"Oh. I don't know. She asked what all our favorite foods were and I told her."

"I hope you said steak." Sport's eyes gleamed.

"I did indeed," said Mr. Rocque.

Sport thought about steak. They could never have steak because it cost too much. A big, thick, juicy steak, and maybe mashed potatoes, and corn and string beans, and sliced tomatoes, and big glasses of milk to wash it all down with; he started to drown in images of food, he wanted it all so badly.

"At least we know it won't be beans," said Mr. Rocque, smiling.

Chapter 7

The doorbell rang. "Gee," said Sport, "you're not dressed." Mr. Rocque got up and went to the door.

"She said not to," he said happily. "She doesn't care what we wear."

He flung open the door, and Sport saw Kate, smiling, with an enormous bag of groceries. Mr. Rocque was holding the door open.

"Take the bag, it's heavy," yelled Sport.

"Oh, here, what am I thinking of?" said Mr. Rocque, coming out of his daze. He grabbed the bag and Kate laughed.

"How're my starving men?" She came into the kitchen.

"God, you bought the A and P," said Mr. Rocque as he put the bag down.

"Just enough to feed two skinny men," said Kate. She pulled an apron out of her purse and put it on. Mr. Rocque was taking things out of the bag. Sport watched everything with fascination, a big grin on his face.

"Look!" said Mr. Rocque, pulling out an enormous slab wrapped in butcher paper. He put it down and unfolded the paper. Sport ran over and together they stared with wonder at the beautiful steak, red and white with tiny white streaks through the red, a great, enormous, beautiful thing. They looked up with wonder to see Kate smiling at them.

"Well, don't eat it raw," she said gently.

"It's *great!*" said Sport and before he knew what he was doing, he had run to her and given her a hug. She laughed down at him, and he gasped with embarrassment and ran from the room. I'll put on a clean shirt, he thought wildly, I'll clean up the living room, I'll . . . nothing was big enough. I know what, he thought immediately. I'll bring out a bottle of Scotch. He crawled under the bed. Carefully hidden under an old sweat shirt, the bottle of Scotch was where he had stored it a year ago. He remembered the day that an old friend of his father's had come to the house bringing three bottles of Scotch as a Christmas present. His father had been out. Sport had taken them, given his father two, and put the third away for some special day. Tonight is special, he thought. Tonight I am happier than I have ever been.

He opened the door to his room and ran to the kitchen, yelling, "Here, here's the surprise," holding the bottle above his head.

Kate was at the sink cleaning vegetables and his father was just reaching for the beer in the icebox. They looked at him in astonishment.

"Here! It's a celebration!" He held out the bottle to them. Kate's eyes were warm and searched his face.

"Where in the devil did you get that?" asked his father.

"Remember that time Mr. Bixley brought you that Scotch?"

"Yes."

"Well, I kept one hidden for some special time."

"This is a special time, son," said Mr. Rocque, "but I don't know how you knew it."

Sport looked at Kate. She continued to look at him with her eyes warm, smiling, almost wet, her mouth in a trembling smile.

"Here," said Mr. Rocque, taking the bottle, "let's drink to a great . . ."

". . . steak," said Kate and smiled at Sport.

"Yeah," said Sport, grinning wildly.

". . . marriage," finished Mr. Rocque and looked at Kate.

Kate looked at Sport.

"What?" said Sport, looking from one to the other.

"I asked Kate to marry me, Sport, and she said yes." Mr. Rocque looked at him patiently.

Sport stood uncertainly, his mouth open, feeling slightly dizzy, not knowing if it were true, or what to say if it were. He stood on the brink of the future and felt himself wavering, feeling completely blank inside. I don't know what marriage means, he thought crazily.

"How about it, son?" said Mr. Rocque quietly, and Sport realized that they were both looking to him for support, like two large children waiting anxiously for his permission to play.

"Kate?" he said uncertainly.

"Yes, darling," she said quietly, and he ran then, ran to grab her in a great unembarrassed hug. She grabbed him up and hugged him back, laughing, then they were all laughing and smiling and crying and they all three hugged at once.

"Well," said Mr. Rocque finally. "Let's drink to *that*!"

"Yes," said Kate, wiping her eyes, "and let me get this dinner on, before my boy gets much skinnier." Sport felt funny inside, skinny and sweet, and felt the words "my boy" like two pats on the head. "I'll have a Coke," he said.

"Good," said his father. "Get your glass, and we'll have a toast."

"There!" said Mr. Rocque as they all clinked glasses.

"To our . . . family!" said Kate.

They all drank. Then they laughed again.

"Now get out of the kitchen, the both of you," said Kate.

"Where will we go?" said Mr. Rocque piteously.

"Into the living room, watch television, read, anything."

"Aw," said Sport.

"Out, out." Kate waved her hands at them. "I mean it."

They went into the living room.

"Set the table, for one thing," called Kate.

They both started to get the things out. "I'll do it," said Sport. Mr. Rocque went and sat down in the living room.

Sport got out the mats, knives and forks, and napkins. He looked at his father, who sat rather stiffly doing nothing. "Why don't you read the paper?" asked Sport.

Mr. Rocque looked surprised, as though this were a brilliant idea. He grabbed the paper like a lifeboat and sat down self-consciously to read it.

Sport finished setting the table, then went and turned on the radio for the news. I am doing what I have seen families do in comic books, he thought quickly. This is the way they behave when there is a man, a woman, and a child. He sat down on a chair. I should be doing homework now, he thought, but I haven't any to do. School doesn't start until Monday. He sat, feeling a kind of peace, a strange sensation of no worry that he had never felt before. He went into his room to be alone.

He closed the door to his room and sat on the edge of his bed. I have a mother. No, he thought hastily, the mother I have is terrible. I have someone else. He thought of Kate in there cooking and his father in there sitting and trying to read the newspaper. He doesn't know what to feel either, he thought sadly, seeing in memory his father's thin shoulders bent over the paper. This will change everything. Where will she hang up her clothes? There aren't enough closets.

Suddenly his mind swirled and he saw his life with his father torn apart like a broken jigsaw puzzle. Where will she hang her clothes? Will we move? Does she know we don't have any money? What will we do with her here? We can't feed her. Not enough money. She *makes* money. A feeling of total confusion overtook him.

He dug his hands into his pockets and tried to restore the reassuring fantasy of a moment ago— Kate in the kitchen, his father protected and loved by someone who would take care of the laundry. . . . But she works, Kate works at a job, how can she do the laundry? If we only had money, he thought again as he had thought every day of his life that he could remember. If we only had money, we would be all right. Does she intend to quit her job? If she does, does she know she'll never see another steak?

But he couldn't really see Kate *having* to have anything, the way his mother *had* to have this, had to have that, as though the world might cave in if she didn't.

Then he heard Kate call, "Dinner's ready," and he thought no more of anything but steak, and bounced out the door, colliding with his father who was rushing to the dinner table.

"When's the last time you fellas ate?" asked Kate, standing at the table, taking off her apron. They laughed and sat down. "Here, darling," said Kate to Mr. Rocque. "Here at the head of the table. Carve the steak."

Mr. Rocque got up, embarrassed, and stood over the steak. He remembered to hold Kate's chair for her, and as she sat she said, "A couple of savages I'm getting."

Sport giggled, then took on a glazed expression as he watched the big pieces of steak his father was putting on each plate. He looked around the table and saw a great bowl of mashed potatoes steaming up around a lump of butter; a plate of big, thick-sliced tomatoes; a bowl of tiny peas, beautiful green tiny peas in butter with little bits of onion in them; a huge platter of corn on the cob; and a basket of hot biscuits.

"There," said Kate, as each person got a plate of

steak. "Now start the bowls around. And take some biscuits while they're hot." Sport grabbed a biscuit and passed the basket. "Take two," said Kate. "You're a big boy."

She poured milk into his glass from the large blue and white pitcher in the middle of the table. It frothed and curled into the glass and he took a huge gulp. She poured from a bottle of red wine she had brought for her and Mr. Rocque.

"There," she said, when all were served. "Bless this house."

"Oh, yes," said Mr. Rocque and raised his glass. They laughed together and then started to eat. Mr. Rocque began to eat fast, cramming in one thing after another.

"Wait a minute," said Kate. "If you eat this way every night, there won't be room for the three of us here."

Sport laughed, looking at his father's face, and then wondered again if she would live there. He didn't care now, only felt the corn against his teeth, the butter running down his chin, the peas, the tomatoes, the mashed potatoes, and the steak. Bless this steak, he thought, and plunged ahead.

"We'll have to do the bedroom over," said Mr. Rocque.

"With . . ." With what, Sport had started to say, then stopped, hoping he had not been heard. He took a gulp of cold milk.

"I've got some things in my apartment that will do fine," said Kate with a sidelong glance at Sport, who gulped harder.

"I don't come with much of a dowry," said Mr. Rocque, laughing.

"Only a head full of books," said Kate, "that will do nicely." She took a bite of steak. Sport noticed that she ate delicately.

That night Sport lay in bed feeling how pleasant it was to have a full stomach. His father and Kate were talking softly in the living room. Soft music came from the radio. Sport lay quietly, listening to new sounds. It may not be true, he said to himself, watch out, it may go away. He fell asleep smiling.

BOOK TWO

Chapter 8

Sport got up in the morning and put on his jeans. He started out into the kitchen, yawning, planning to make the coffee as usual, and was confronted by the smell of bacon frying. "Wow," he said under his breath. He went into the kitchen. Kate stood at the stove.

"Good morning," she said, smiling.

"Good morning," said Sport, and grinned from ear to ear.

"Sit down. Breakfast'll be ready in a minute. The only thing I don't know is . . . what do boys drink for breakfast?"

"Coffee," said Sport, looking at her in wonder. The whole kitchen seemed different, not closed up, unused, not smelling of last night's dishes the way it usually did when he came in in the morning. This morning everything was clean, smelled great, seemed to be filled with a yellow light. Kate wore a yellow dress.

"That doesn't seem right," she was saying. "I would have thought milk."

"We don't have enough milk," said Sport.

"Oh yes we do," said Kate, and going to the refrigerator, she opened the door and showed him two bottles. "And after today it's going to be delivered. It's cheaper that way and it's better milk. Do you *like* milk for breakfast?" she asked.

"Sure," said Sport.

She poured him an enormous glass. He gulped it.

"Easy," she said lightly. "More coming up here." She hummed a little to herself as she made scrambled eggs. "I hate to bring up an unpleasant subject," she said, smiling at him as she turned the eggs, "but when does school start?"

"Monday," said Sport. "That's four days from now."

"Well, no one had mentioned it. I was just curious." She piled eggs on a plate, added four slices of bacon, reached in the oven, took out two hot rolls, put them on the plate, and handed the whole thing to Sport. He couldn't believe his eyes.

"It's like dinner," he said wonderingly.

"Eat. Dinner, he says. Wait'll he sees dinner." Kate smiled at him and went back to the stove.

He started to eat. He started to eat very fast. He had never realized how hungry he could be in the morning.

"Take it easy," said Kate, sitting down opposite

him with only a cup of coffee. "There's tomorrow morning, too, and the morning after and so forth."

"What?" said Sport.

"Never mind, eat," said Kate and laughed.

The phone rang. Sport kept on eating until it rang again and he realized that Kate hadn't answered it. He looked at her. She looked at him. She had started to get up but looked uncertain.

"Want me to get it?" asked Sport.

"I think you better," said Kate.

He jumped up and ran to the phone.

"Hello?" he said into the mouthpiece.

"Hello," a woman's voice bellowed at him. "Is this the residence of Matthew Rocque?"

"Yes," said Sport, wondering what she was screaming at and having a faint memory of having heard her voice before, an unpleasant memory.

"Is Mr. Rocque in, please?" yelled the voice.

"Yes," said Sport, "but he's asleep. Can I take a message?"

"Asleep?" screamed the woman, and Sport suddenly recognized her. She was the nurse who had yelled at him over his grandfather's bed. "He can be awakened," she cried. "Mr. Vane has passed away."

"What?" said Sport. She was yelling so loud he couldn't hear her.

"Mr. Vane has died," she shouted.

"Oh," said Sport.

"Is this Simon?" she asked, her voice dropping an octave.

"Yes," said Sport.

"Simon. You must come right away. Your grandfather has gone to heaven."

"Oh," said Sport, thinking, What do I have to go for, if he's already left for heaven?

"Wake your father." She was shouting again. "Your mother needs you now. Come over here." The phone seemed to tumble out of her hands on the other end as there was a crash and then a click.

Sport hung up. He went back into the kitchen. Kate was looking at him, but she didn't say anything. He sat down.

"Grandfather died."

"Oh, dear," said Kate.

Sport said nothing; he picked up his fork and started to eat again. The food didn't taste the same. He felt that perhaps he shouldn't be eating, but he wanted to, all the same.

"Did you like him?" asked Kate.

"Sort of," said Sport. He shoved a roll in his mouth.

"Was he a nice man?"

"I don't know. He was nice to me."

"Does . . . did your father like him?" Kate seemed tentative.

"I guess so," said Sport. He could think of nothing beyond the fact that the nurse had yelled at him to come over there. I don't want to go over there. I don't ever want to go over there. Ever. If he's dead, then there's no reason to go.

"He doesn't like my mother," said Sport suddenly, and looked at Kate.

Kate smiled. "Want some more?" she said gently, looking at his empty plate.

"What? No," said Sport. "Uh . . . no, thanks."

She smiled and took his plate to the sink to wash it.

"Who called?" she asked as she came back with a new cup of coffee.

"The nurse," said Sport. "She says we have to go over there."

"Oh?"

"I guess I better wake up Dad."

"I guess so," said Kate. "I've got to be going to work. It's a shame . . ."

"Well," said Sport, "he was old."

"No, I mean"—she looked at him and smiled—"it's a shame because your father wanted to work today. Now he'll have to go over there."

"Yeah," said Sport. He knew his father hated appointments more than anything in the world. All I ask of the world, his father had said more than once, is just one day after another with nothing planned.

Sport got up.

"I'll wake him," said Kate quickly and stood up.

Sport looked at her and sat down again.

She went into his father's room. His father groaned as he heard the door open.

In a few minutes his father appeared in the doorway. He smiled at Sport and rubbed his head. Kate was behind him. She went to the stove.

"Here," she said, "a cup of coffee first. Before anything," she added, and looked at Sport.

Don't look at me, he thought, I don't want to tell him anyway.

His father sat down and gulped the hot coffee. He looked up at Kate and grinned foolishly. Kate smiled at him. He gulped more coffee. "Well," he said finally, "that's more like it." She got up and poured him some more coffee. He looked around and smiled at everybody.

"Well, now," he said. "What's everybody doing today?"

"I'm going to work," said Kate.

"So am I," said Mr. Rocque very definitely and very happily.

"Uh, Dad," said Sport.

"Darling," began Kate, "someone called this morning and . . ." She looked at Sport.

"Well, what is it?" said Mr. Rocque.

"Gramps died," said Sport quickly.

"Oh . . . oh, yeah?" said Mr. Rocque sadly, looking at each of them in turn. "He was a nice old geezer," he said and shook his head.

"They want us to come over there," said Sport after a minute.

"What for?" asked Mr. Rocque, beginning to sound outraged.

"I don't know," said Sport.

"Who called?"

"The nurse."

"What does she know? What could they want?"

"Perhaps," said Kate, "they need some help with arrangements."

"With all that money?" snorted Mr. Rocque.

"Maybe there's no man to do it all," said Kate.

"There's Wilton, his lawyer, any number of people," said Mr. Rocque grumpily.

"Well," said Kate, "I'm off to work." She stood up.

"Aw," said Mr. Rocque.

Kate ran a hand over his head. "I'll see you two tonight. Any ideas for supper?"

"Steak," said Sport.

They both looked at him and laughed. "Steak it is," said Kate. She got her coat, waved to them, and was gone. The door closing after her made them both feel empty.

"Damn!" said Mr. Rocque.

"What?" said Sport.

"I wanted to work."

"Work anyway," said Sport eagerly. He didn't want to go either.

"Can't."

"Why?"

"There must be some reason I'm needed there."

"Call 'em up and see."

"Yeah," said Mr. Rocque. "Maybe I can do it all over the phone."

Mr. Rocque got up and placed the call. He muttered so low into the receiver that Sport couldn't hear anything. He came back into the kitchen, poured himself some more coffee, and sat down heavily.

"Have to go over," he said.

"Why?"

"Oh, have to make arrangements for the funeral."

"Why can't Mr. Wilton?"

"He's out of town."

"Why can't Mother?"

Mr. Rocque looked at his son. "If there's a man around, women don't do that kind of thing."

"Why?" asked Sport.

His father looked at him. "That's a very intelligent question, son. I'm not sure, but I would say offhand that in this culture, when there's responsibility to be taken, men are supposed to take it."

"Oh," said Sport.

"It's part of supporting a woman," Mr. Rocque said rather uncertainly. "It's part of a man's job."

"But Kate works," said Sport. He thought of Mrs. O'Neil, who worked. The only women he knew who didn't work were his mother and Harry's mother.

"Aaagh," said Mr. Rocque deep in his throat. "The trouble is, Sport, you have an unusual father. I do not go out to a job like ordinary men. We do not live in an ordinary way. Now, the normal, ordinary thing is that the man goes to work and supports the woman, takes over all outside responsibility, and in turn the woman runs the house."

"But you're not married to Mother anymore."

"True," said Mr. Rocque. "Very true," he said slowly and seemed to disappear somewhere inside himself.

They sat for a minute in silence. Mr. Rocque scratched his head once. He leaned forward finally and said, "I guess the thing is, when you've once been married to someone, you retain a certain feeling of friendship. I know that your mother is incapable of getting this done, and it has to be done."

Sport nodded.

"Someone has to do it," said Mr. Rocque, sitting back.

"But how can you be friends with someone so mean?" Sport burst out.

Mr. Rocque looked at him. "I don't mean friends like you and Seymour or you and Harry. I mean friends with someone you've once had a son with."

He smiled. "You'll understand later, although I hope the situation never arises."

Sport jumped when he heard the words "had a son with." He never could seem to remember that his mother was really his mother.

"I hope that you get married and stay married and that you and your wife really care for each other and that she is nice."

"Like Kate?"

"Yes," said Mr. Rocque and broke into a big grin. "Like Kate."

Sport looked away. His father was grinning in such a silly way that it embarrassed him. "Why do I have to go over there?" he asked his father.

"You don't," said his father. "Who said you did?"

"The nurse."

"Frizzle the nurse. I say you don't." His father stood up. "Do what you like today. School starts soon. Which reminds me. Your mother was going to take you and buy you some clothes this weekend. I don't know if she still wants to. I'll ask her when I see her."

"Oh, no," said Sport.

His father laughed at his morose expression, then left to get dressed.

Chapter 9

Mr. Rocque was gone all day. When he got back that night, Kate was already there cooking dinner.

"Well, how'd it go?" she said brightly as he came into the kitchen.

"Woof," said Mr. Rocque.

"Bad?" asked Kate.

"How about a drink?" said Mr. Rocque. Sport had never seen him so grumpy.

"You look like you could use it," said Kate. She put ice and Scotch into a glass and handed it to him.

Mr. Rocque took a long swallow, made a face as though it tasted terrible, then let out a long sigh. "You know," he said slowly, "if you *have* to die, and we have to die, you'd think it would be easier to die rich."

Kate looked at him. "It is," she said simply.

"Well, yeah. But on the other hand, now picture this. I go to the house and Charlotte is there sobbing dutifully, and Carrie is there putting on a very tidy show of hysterics. I say, okay, I'm going over to the funeral home now, and they both look up through their tears and practically in unison they say, 'Not too expensive a casket.' I haven't, naturally, a price list of caskets on me, so I say, 'What would you like? A nice pine box?' and they're both horrified. 'Something suitable,' says Carrie demurely. 'No one will see it anyway,' says Charlotte. 'It will be covered with flowers.' I see she has in mind a longish orange crate. 'Randolph's was very nice,' says Carrie. Randolph is her husband who is dead some four years. 'I got Randolph's for two thousand,' she says, as though she got it on sale at Macy's."

"It's incredible," said Kate.

"So," Mr. Rocque continued, "I say, 'Shall I try for two thousand?' and Charlotte looks at me and bursts into tears. 'You always were brutal,' she says to me!"

"I don't believe it," said Kate.

"Brutal! Are you ready for that?" Mr. Rocque poured himself another drink and sat down again. "They're sitting there bargaining, and I'm brutal. So I leave. I go to the funeral home. Some man ushers me into a room full of caskets. I look at them. You could go to Europe in some of them, first class. They've got silver handles, gold even. He points to one that looks so much like a Mercedes, I get out of the way. He says, 'This is very nice.' I feel like saying, 'Listen, the guy's dead, he won't be able to trade it in next year,' but I say nothing and ask the price. He says ten thousand. Are you ready?"

"Ten thousand dollars?!" yelled Sport.

"That's right," said Mr. Rocque.

"They're ridiculous," said Kate.

"Now here's the payoff. That's the lowest price they have." Mr. Rocque looked around triumphantly.

"No," said Kate.

"What'd you do then?" asked Sport.

"I say, very softly, because I don't want to hurt him, I say, 'I think I'm in the wrong room.' He looks very sad. I say, 'We're interested in something a little less expensive.' He looks even sadder. 'It will be covered anyway,' I say desperately, and he looks like he will cry. We stand there at a loss. I am not going to give in and he is not going to give in."

"What happened then?" said Kate.

"We'd still be standing there if Wilton hadn't walked in."

"I thought he was out of town," said Sport.

"He was, but not far, evidently. He got the news and came right back. Well, when he walks in, the whole thing changes. He doesn't even say hello to the guy, who is now wringing his hands like he's got poison ivy. Wilton marches up to him, nods at me, and says, 'Five thousand.' The one in the black suit glides like with roller skates right over to an exact duplicate of the Mercedes and points to it. Wilton nods and that's the end of it. We walk out."

"Fascinating," said Kate.

"Five thousand dollars!" yelled Sport.

Mr. Rocque looked at him and laughed. "Look at the accountant," he said fondly.

"Seymour's father's cost three thousand," said Sport.

"They will arrive at their intended destinations no matter what it costs," said Mr. Rocque.

"No matter what you're driving," said Kate and they laughed. "What a day you've had," she continued.

"Interesting. Very interesting," said Mr. Rocque. "Now, we go back to the house. We all go into the library and have tea. Charlotte is dying to see the will, but doesn't want to ask, so she thinks of ways to use the word *will* in a sentence. If she can't do that, she manages to work in the word *inheritance*. Wilton just sips his tea. Carrie can't stand it and finally says, 'When can we hear the will?' Wilton, cool as a cucumber, says, 'I have the will with me. I intend to read it to you. I wondered, however,' and then he looks at me, 'whether you wanted the primary beneficiary to be here.' I look back at him because I don't know what he is talking about, and

Charlotte screams. 'What are you talking about?'
she yells like a fishwife. 'Perhaps he is too young,'
says Wilton and opens his briefcase. At this point
Carrie faints."

"Does all this mean what I think it does?" asked
Kate.

"Yes," said Mr. Rocque and they both looked
at Sport.

"What does it mean?" asked Sport nervously.

"Tell it the way it happened," said Kate. She
poured herself and Mr. Rocque a drink and then
sat down at the table.

"Well, some smelling salts are brought to Carrie,
then Wilton starts reading the will. I don't want
to go into the whole thing because, you know, it's
endless, but just the principal thing, which is this:
Carrie is left out altogether. Charlotte gets one
fourth of the estate, and the residual estate is
left entirely to Sport."

"What?" Sport yelled.

"Wow!" said Kate.

"Rather gives you a turn, doesn't it?" said Mr.
Rocque quietly.

"You mean me?" shouted Sport. "Me? I get the
money?"

"Yes," said Mr. Rocque.

Sport's eyes got enormous. "But I'm only a little
kid," he said finally. Money, I have money. Where
is it? he thought crazily.

"As far as he was concerned, you were the only son he ever had. He hated women, old man Vane, just hated them."

"I don't believe it," said Sport. "Where is it? Where's the money?"

"It is kind of hard to believe," said Kate.

"It's more complicated, son, than just being handed some money. It's in trust for you until you're thirty-five. He picked that age, I'm sure, because he always said a man didn't know anything until he was thirty-five, and a woman never knew anything."

"Oh," said Sport and felt mysteriously relieved.

"Now this is the peculiar part," said Mr. Rocque. "It's in trust, which means only the income comes to you, and the two trustees are me and Charlotte."

"Whoops," said Kate.

"Exactly," said Mr. Rocque. "Do you understand what that means, Sport?"

"I understand the income from the capital comes to me," said Sport, "but the capital doesn't until I'm thirty-five. But I don't understand what a trustee is."

"Boy, are you smart," said Kate, impressed. "I didn't know what all those words meant until I was thirty." She laughed at herself. "And a lot of it I still don't understand."

"He's got a head for this that won't quit," said Mr. Rocque. "I think you got it from old man Vane, because you never got it from me." Mr. Rocque took a swallow of his drink and continued. "The thing is this. I said that Charlotte got one fourth. Well, that's true, but if she stays here, keeps you for half the year, acts as a trustee, and generally behaves like a responsible woman, she gets one half."

"Oh, dear," said Kate.

"You mean I have to live with her?" asked Sport in horror.

"For half the year," said Mr. Rocque. "But I'm betting she won't do it. I think she'll try, but I think she'll ultimately decide that the one fourth is enough for her, especially when she doesn't have to have any responsibility."

"I don't want to live with her," said Sport. "Tell them I don't want the money. I'd rather not have the money and live with you."

Mr. Rocque looked at his son. Sport's face was set in a mask of horror. "You can't give it back, son. There's no one to give it back to."

"Why not?" yelled Sport. "Why would you make me live with her?"

"Wait a minute. Whoa," said Mr. Rocque. "Take it easy now. I'm not making you. When the court decided the custody case, that's the way it was decided, that you should live with me half the year and with your mother the other half. Up until now she has lived out of the country precisely because she didn't want to have anything to do with bringing up a child. She still isn't going to want to."

"Why did he write the will this way?" asked Kate.

"Because . . ." Mr. Rocque thought a minute. ". . . I think that he wanted Charlotte to be a good mother. You know, old man Vane never had a mother. His mother died when he was very young and he always said that it was the hardest thing in the world, growing up without a mother. I think he saw Sport growing up the same way and decided to do something about it. He knows his daughter. He knew very well that greed would be the only thing in the world that could make her take on the responsibility. And so he's set it up where she has to, to get half of the money. If she ultimately wants to give that up and take only the one fourth with no child attached, then she can do that, too. I am sure she will do the latter." He looked at Sport as he said this. "I can almost promise you, son," he said gently.

"But suppose she doesn't?" said Sport. He felt like crying. Here everything was, nice and happy, with Kate in the house, and he would have to move out for half the year.

"What was Charlotte's reaction to the will?" asked Kate.

"Terrible, as you can imagine," said Mr. Rocque, "She's furious. After Carrie was roused from her second faint, she and Charlotte both began to mutter about 'undue influence' and 'breaking the will.' Wilton put a stop to it immediately. He told them they wouldn't have a chance in the world."

"What did she do then?" asked Sport.

"It wasn't pretty," said Mr. Rocque. "She turned sort of purple with rage and started to scream all sorts of things."

"Like what?" asked Kate.

"Oh, that she doesn't want to take care of any child . . ."

"Good," said Sport. "She doesn't have to."

"Precisely," said Mr. Rocque. "Now you're beginning to see what I mean. Her character is absolutely unfit for having you around and she is going to do everything in her power not to. She knows she has to take you shopping for clothes tomorrow, and she acted absolutely martyred about it."

"Why can't I just buy my clothes around here?" asked Sport.

"Oh, but then you wouldn't look like her son," said Mr. Rocque, laughing. "And besides, she has to buy you a suit to wear to the funeral, which is day after tomorrow. And there everyone will know you're her son, so you've got to look good."

"Oh, geez," said Sport.

"How about some dinner?" said Kate, getting up and going to the stove.

"Great," said Mr. Rocque. "I'm starved."

Sport looked at his father. You don't have to move somewhere else, he thought bitterly. I'm not even hungry. He felt his eyes begin to fill with tears.

He went into his own room and sat on the bed. In a minute his father knocked on the door.

"What?" said Sport.

"I'd like to talk to you," said his father through the door.

"All right," said Sport.

His father came in and closed the door behind him. He didn't look at Sport, but went over and sat at Sport's desk. Looking out of the window, he began to talk.

"This is all a great shock to everyone, son. It isn't a pleasant situation, to say the least. The only pleasant thing about it is that you will have enough to live on the rest of your life, and when you're thirty-five, you'll be a multimillionaire."

Sport turned the words over in his mouth. Multimillionaire. Multimillionaire. They brought to mind pictures in advertisements of a chauffeur getting a case of whiskey out of a Rolls-Royce.

"But, Dad . . ." he began.

"Just a minute, son. Let me finish." Mr. Rocque spoke quietly and continued to look out the window. "I don't know much, and God knows I don't make any money, but a writer at least knows one thing, and that is character. I know your mother's character like the back of my hand. I know that she will not go through with this.

"She will give it a try, because she's greedy, but she will hate it, and she'll never be able to keep it up. She will quit and she will go back to Europe and everything will be exactly the way it was before, except that you will have more money."

"*We* will have more money," said Sport rather nervously.

"I am a trustee of your money, Sport. I'm not getting the money, you are," Mr. Rocque said patiently.

"Well, what does that mean?" said Sport, trying to keep from yelling. "You mean I'm gonna be living on steak while you eat beans?"

"No," said Mr. Rocque, laughing. "I imagine we can get a better apartment, live better. After thirty-five, maybe you'll support me. . . ." He laughed, his eyes shining.

Sport laughed.

His father cleared his throat, stood up. "How about some steak?"

"Yeah," said Sport and laughed. "What do we need money for anyway? We got steak already."

Chapter 10

The next morning, after Kate had left for work, Sport and his father were sitting at the breakfast table. Mr. Rocque was having a last cup of coffee before going to work in his study.

"You look sleepy," he said. "Didn't you sleep well?"

"Oh, yeah," said Sport.

"Too much excitement in one day," said Mr. Rocque. "When you get back this afternoon, maybe you should grab a nap before dinner."

"A *nap*," said Sport. "I'm eleven years old. I haven't had a nap since I was six."

"I'm forty-five," said Mr. Rocque. "And I plan to have one this afternoon. When this much happens all at once, you find you get tired."

"Hmmmph," said Sport. "What time am I going?"

"The car is picking you up at eleven. You're going to Brooks Brothers and then to lunch."

"What for? I can have lunch here."

"Because after lunch you're going someplace else for shoes."

"Oh, geez," said Sport.

"Go on, now. Put a clean shirt on and your suit."

"The arms are too short."

"That's what you're going for, to get one where the arms aren't too short. Now, hop. She'll be mad as a snake if you're late, and I don't want her up here yelling at me."

I don't want her up here either, thought Sport and went to his room. The only clean shirt he had was red-and-white checked. He took a shower and put on the shirt and his gray suit, feeling sad and heavy the whole time.

At eleven, he yelled good-bye to his father and went down the steps. The long black car was just pulling up to the curb. As he came down the front steps of his house, he caught a glimpse of his mother in the backseat. She seemed to have furs pulled up to her chin.

Egbert, the chauffeur, jumped out of the front seat and ran around the car. He opened the back door and Sport stepped in. He was assaulted by his mother's perfume.

"Good morning," she said coldly, looking him up and down. "I see you *do* need a suit. Or did your father have you put on the oldest one?" She gave a bitter laugh.

"I only have one suit," said Sport. He punched the button to roll down the window to get away from the perfume.

"What are you doing? It's cold." Charlotte pushed the button on her side with one quick, furious finger.

"It doesn't seem cold." Sport watched the window close.

His mother didn't seem to hear him. It wasn't cold. The perfume was sickening. Oh, swell, he thought to himself, I'll throw up all over Brooks Brothers.

"One suit." She snorted. "Does your father teach you to make these pitiful little cries or do you think they're amusing?"

"What?" said Sport.

"Never mind. With your money you can keep the neighborhood in suits."

Sport thought of Harry, who must have twenty suits since he worked after school and spent every cent on clothes. Seymour had the same blue suit he'd had for years because he hadn't gotten much taller.

His mother lapsed into silence. He stared out the window. They were going down the East River Drive. The tugboats were all up and down the river. The sun was so bright, it hurt his eyes.

At Forty-ninth they turned off the drive past the apartment building that had just gone up next to the United Nations.

"Now there's a nice place," said Charlotte. "I think I may move in there. Billie Cleever got two floors there and the view is sensational."

"Two floors?" said Sport.

She ignored him again. "I don't know. The old house is a pretty place. Perhaps I won't sell it."

"Are you going to stay in America?" asked Sport.

"Turn here," she said into the speaking tube which connected with the glassed-in driver's seat. "Drop us here on the corner. And come back at one o'clock sharp."

The car stopped in front of the door to Brooks Brothers. Charlotte took her sweet time getting out. Horns were blowing wildly. Drivers were screaming and a policeman was walking lazily toward them when she finally turned toward the building. "One o'clock sharp," she said to Egbert, and they went in the door.

"Ah, Miss Vane," said a terribly thin man with sparse hair.

"Yes," said Charlotte and swept past him to the elevators. Sport looked back to see the man standing with his mouth open.

Charlotte got into a waiting elevator. "Boys," she said, as though the word turned her stomach.

The elevator zoomed up and the doors opened.

Charlotte stepped off and was immediately affronted by the number of people in the boys' department. "What in the world is this?" she said loudly.

"Ah, Miss Vane," said a short, slim, tiny-footed man in exactly the same voice as the man downstairs.

"What *is* all this?" said Charlotte, watching the mothers hustling sons into jackets, fathers picking up overcoats and putting them on boys.

"Ah! Back to school," said the man. "You usually pay your visit somewhat later." He tiptoed down the aisle in front of Charlotte.

"Here, I know exactly what I want for him." She pointed to Sport, who felt like a fish in a tank as the man turned a squinted eye on him and looked him up and down. Too small, throw it back, flashed through Sport's mind.

"Umm, yes. Do we want school clothes?" he chirruped, squinting harder than ever.

"The first thing I need is something for a funeral," said Charlotte crisply, her eyes flicking with distaste over the other women in the department.

"Aaagh." The man seemed caught between an expression of sympathy and a cough. He stopped squinting and stared at Charlotte.

"Quickly now," she said sharply, her eyes suddenly focusing on him. "I have a luncheon engagement."

He jumped. "Yes, aagh. Black. A black suit. Perhaps dark gray." He hesitated.

How about red? thought Sport.

"Gray," said Charlotte. "Much more sensible. Although black might be chic."

And a nice homburg to go with it, Sport said to himself.

The salesman's eyes squinted again as he watched Charlotte. He looked at Sport. "Is he growing very fast?" he asked.

"Who knows?" said Charlotte, making the salesman's eyebrows hop. "Why quibble? Two suits, then, a black and a nice gray, light gray. I don't like dark gray, it looks Jewish."

"Whatever that means," said Sport in spite of himself. Seymour was Jewish and he'd never had a gray suit in his life.

"Certainly, madam," said the salesman and disappeared.

Sport was seething. "What do you mean, Jewish?" he said loudly. Several women turned around.

"Shut up!" said Charlotte. She pushed a child aside and went to the shirt counter. A man with very blond hair said, "Yes?"

"I want four white, two blue, one pink, one

yellow, one blue-striped, one gray-striped. No, two blue-striped. Very nice."

"Size?" said the blond man who looked as though he hated her. Sport smiled to himself.

"They're for her," he said happily to the man, who smiled at him, a white-toothed, genuine grin.

Charlotte had not even heard him. "Here he is," she said, grabbing Sport somewhere around the middle of the back and shoving him into the counter.

"Let's try a thirteen," said the man. He took out a shirt and unbuttoned it. Sport took off his jacket.

"Good Lord! Where did you get that awful shirt?" said Charlotte.

"My father and I got it at Melnikoff's on York Avenue," said Sport. He was laughing now because the blond man had come around the counter and was winking at him behind his mother's back.

He put the shirt on and it fit.

"Good," said Charlotte. "I suppose you don't have pajamas," she said shortly.

"I don't wear pajamas," said Sport.

"Four pairs of pajamas," said Charlotte.

"Socks," she said to no one in particular. She picked out socks.

The man with the suits came back. Charlotte looked at the material. "Fine," she said briefly.

"If you'll step in here," said the Squinter, nudging Sport with a hanger. "We'll have them fitted right away." Sport turned and followed the man.

"Put an overcoat on him," said Charlotte loudly.

"Certainly, madam," cooed the Squinter and pushed Sport into a booth.

"Underwear," Sport could hear Charlotte say loudly through the curtain.

After the suits were fitted, Sport tried on two overcoats and Charlotte decided on both.

The pile of clothes on the counter was immense, and both the Squinter and the blond man looked happy. "Send them all except one white shirt and the black suit, which my chauffeur will pick up after lunch."

Sport followed his mother to the elevator.

"There," said Charlotte, pulling on her gloves. "Now for a very cold martini." For some reason this made her look at Sport and smile. She seemed suddenly relaxed.

"Are you going to stay in America?" said Sport quickly, hoping to catch her in a receptive mood.

"Here's the elevator," said Charlotte and they walked in.

Even when she's happy she doesn't hear me, thought Sport. Maybe I don't talk loud enough.

"Are you going to stay in America?" he said in a great booming voice.

"Sssh," said Charlotte. The elevator was full of

people. When it got to the main floor she took his arm and shoved him.

"Don't talk loud in elevators," she hissed in his ear. "You sound like a Jew."

"Oh, for God's sake," yelled Sport, but she was already ahead of him going out the door.

Chapter 11

The funeral was at eleven o'clock the next morning. At ten Sport was in his new suit. Kate turned him around and around in admiration. He grinned, embarrassed. She held him off for a last look and said, "I was going to say, you'll knock 'em dead, but I guess that's not appropriate, is it?"

"A little too close," said Mr. Rocque, coming into the living room.

"My, you don't look half bad yourself," said Kate.

"It's not exactly a new suit," said Mr. Rocque, rubbing his head and grinning in a lopsided way.

"It's exactly eight years old," said Sport.

"That would make you three when he bought it. How can you remember that?" asked Kate as she straightened Mr. Rocque's tie and brushed off his jacket.

"I don't," said Sport. "I just remember that three years ago when he wanted to buy a new one he said it was five years old."

"How long *have* you been handling his finances?" asked Kate, looking at Sport with a curious expression.

"He leaped from the womb with a ledger," said Mr. Rocque.

"Lucky for you," said Kate. "Where would you be today without him?"

"Ah, but where would he be without me?" said Mr. Rocque.

They laughed at his serious face. "Come on, now. We've got to be going."

"I thought it wasn't until eleven," said Kate. She looked sad.

"Oh, poor darling," said Mr. Rocque. "She gets a Saturday off and what do we do? Go off to a jolly funeral and leave her all alone."

"What do we have to do there?" asked Sport. I don't know what to do at a funeral, he thought. I hope I don't have to look at any corpse. Seymour said you have to look at the corpse.

"You just stick right next to me and do what I do," said Mr. Rocque. "Come on, let's go."

Kate waved at them from the top of the stairs. Sport looked down at his new suit. It must have cost a lot, he thought. I hope I see Harry. I'll show him.

They took a cab to the funeral parlor, for which Sport was thankful. Going to a funeral was bad enough, but being driven there by Mr. Rocque would have been worse.

"It's in a funeral parlor instead of a church because Mr. Vane hated churches," said Mr. Rocque on the way over. "There will be a short service, and then we'll go in limousines to the cemetery. Charlotte didn't even want me along, of course, but I said that if I weren't there, I wouldn't let you come."

"Gee, yeah," said Sport, thinking in horror of going alone.

"Now there's one thing," said Mr. Rocque and hesitated. "The casket will be closed, except for the family."

"What does that mean?" asked Sport.

"If the family wishes to view the body before the services, it may. The casket will then be closed," Mr. Rocque said uncomfortably.

"You mean look at a dead body?" said Sport loudly.

"Well, that's why I wanted to tell you this before we got there. It's going to come up, so I wanted to know how you felt about it."

"How do you feel about it?" asked Sport weakly.

"I think it's barbaric," said Mr. Rocque. "On the other hand, it's an experience you've never had. Not that I think every experience is valuable, by any means."

"I don't want to see any body," said Sport.

"Okay. That's settled. You won't."

They arrived at the funeral home. A large crowd was gathered in front, and long black limousines were parked at the curb in front and around the corner. Sport began to shake. Mr. Rocque paid the cab driver and they got out.

As they were going in, Sport saw Charlotte and Carrie get out of the car. Egbert held the door open as they swept out, both covered in black veils.

They went in. The front room was cool. A man in a brown suit with pimples on his face ushered them into a little room. The lights were very low, and Sport couldn't see anything at first. Then, across a length of sea-green carpet, past great wreaths of white flowers, he saw an open casket. He grabbed his father's hand.

The door opened noiselessly, and Charlotte and Carrie came in. They looked like a spook movie.

Charlotte stuck out a black glove at Mr. Rocque as though she'd just met him. The black lump that was Carrie waddled over and stuck out its black glove. A sniffle came out from under her veil. They floated past and into the room that had the body.

Sport watched as they stood a few minutes, leaning against each other and looking down. Charlotte's shoulders started to shake under the black veil. Carrie clutched her arm.

The door opened silently. It's like a ship, thought Sport, with an underwater pressure-cabin. The pimply man in the brown suit glided in and whispered something in Mr. Rocque's ear. Mr. Rocque was already going out the door.

Sport stood not knowing what to do with his hands.

Carrie suddenly glided over to him, swiftly took his hand, and pulled him into the other room. Before he knew what was happening to him, he was looking down at a yellow wax image of Grandfather Vane with his teeth in. It doesn't look like him, he thought, as one would say of a bad portrait. Carrie was wringing his hand in her own clammy one and snuffling. He looked at the long hands, folded, the neat suit. Who tied the tie? he wondered.

Mr. Rocque came into the room, was across the floor in two bounds, jerked Sport's hand out of Carrie's, propelled him across the floor and out the door into another room. Carrie and Charlotte followed.

This room was better lighted. It was a small chapel with an altar and candles. All four of them were ushered into seats behind a kind of latticework partition, through which they could see the services but not be seen by the other mourners. The chapel began to fill.

Music started. Charlotte started to cry. Carrie

cried even louder. Mr. Rocque looked straight ahead at nothing. Sport did the same. All he could think of was that wax doll in the box.

The minister began to speak. He droned on and on. Sport didn't hear a word he said. He thought of Grandfather Vane and how he had liked him.

It was finally over, and the people in the chapel moved out one door as the four of them moved out another. They found themselves on the street being ushered into a limousine.

Charlotte said once, "Can I smoke?"

Carrie said, "Better not."

The long black car pulled away like a ship gliding away from dock. It didn't make any noise at all. No one made any noise. Sport began to itch all over.

They went out on the Long Island Expressway. No one spoke for the entire ride. They pulled into the cemetery. Winding back through it, the car stopped in front of a small pavilion which had been erected next to a mound of dirt. People were running around setting up flowers. The pall-bearers stood around next to the car from the funeral home. The four of them sat in the car until the pallbearers had hoisted the coffin onto their shoulders and then onto a rack which was suspended over the open grave.

They then got out of the car and started up a

steep little hill. Mr. Rocque helped Carrie and
Sport try to stand up to get away from Charlotte,
who was leaning on his arm.

When they sat down in front of the grave, Sport
realized that the seats were on such a slant that it
was impossible to stay on them. He just slid off.
He slid into Charlotte, who started sliding toward
Carrie. Mr. Rocque put out his foot to stop them
all, and Charlotte gave Sport a look through her
veil. It's a good thing we're going sideways,
thought Sport, or we'd all end up in the grave.

The minister was droning again. He droned for
what seemed like two hours and then he stopped.
They all got up and went into the car again, the
other people waiting until they had gone by. The
car started off.

Charlotte threw off her veil. "That's that," she
said with a great sigh of relief as she lit a
cigarette. The expression on her face was the first
thing Sport had ever liked about her.

"A beautiful funeral," said Carrie. "Simply
beautiful."

"Hmmmm," said Mr. Rocque.

"Wasn't it lovely, dear?" said Carrie, looking
through her veil at Sport.

"Peachy," said Sport.

"What?" said Carrie.

Mr. Rocque gave Sport a look.

"Yes, ma'am," said Sport.

"Oh, I thought it was just lovely," continued Carrie. "They certainly do a good job."

"Yes," said Mr. Rocque.

"And such nice-looking people they hire," said Carrie.

Sport thought of the pimply man in the brown suit.

"And such a lovely cemetery." Carrie gave a sigh of pleasure.

You'd think she'd been to a Broadway show, thought Sport.

No one said anything then until they got back to the funeral home.

"My car is waiting," said Charlotte. She and Carrie got out. "We can drop you," she said, sticking her head back into the window.

"No, thank you," said Mr. Rocque, scrambling out. Sport got out as fast as he could.

Mr. Rocque hailed a cab and they jumped in. He gave the address and then leaned back and let out an enormous sigh. "Jesus," he said finally.

"Yeah," said Sport.

"Hey, son." Mr. Rocque sat up and slapped Sport on the knee. "How would you like to go out to dinner?"

"Have we got any money?" asked Sport.

"Yes," said Mr. Rocque.

"How much?" asked Sport.

"Oh, thirty million," said Mr. Rocque and laughed. "No, seriously, I got my royalty check today."

"Oh, yeah?" Sport felt happy.

"Maybe we could go to that great Chinese restaurant on East End," said Mr. Rocque.

"That's expensive," said Sport in a worried voice.

"Don't worry," said Mr. Rocque. He looked at Sport. "The least you can carry away from all this mess is the feeling that you don't have to worry about money."

I haven't seen any money yet, thought Sport, and until I do, I won't believe it.

"Well," said Mr. Rocque, "Monday you start school."

"Yeah. A new one, too." Sport thought of all the people he had gone to school with at the Gregory School. Pinky Whitehead, Harriet Welsch, Janie Gibbs, Beth Ellen Hansen. They were mostly girls because the Gregory School was a girls' school, but boys were allowed to attend through the sixth grade. Sport was going into the seventh grade and so he was going to public school this year. Seymour and Harry would be in his class. He wondered if it would be easier or harder than the other school and whether he would make friends or not.

"And then next weekend, we've got a big weekend coming up," said Mr. Rocque with obvious joy in his voice.

"Yeah, what?"

"Kate and I are getting married next weekend."

Chapter 12

On Monday Sport started off for school. He and his father and Kate had gone out to the Chinese restaurant on Saturday night. On Sunday they had made plans for the wedding, which was on Friday. Kate and his father would be married at City Hall and then come back to the apartment for a party. His father had invited all his friends and Kate had invited all hers.

The only thing bad about the whole thing was that on Saturday his father and Kate were going to the beach for a week, and Sport would have to stay with his mother. He had already decided that if he didn't like it, he would sneak back to the apartment and live alone. He had done it once before when his father had had to be out of town, and he was perfectly capable of taking care of himself. He had told his father that last night, but his father had said that it was for the best because the quicker Charlotte got a dose of having a kid around, the quicker she'd leave town.

Sport walked along East End Avenue. His school was down at Seventy-eighth and York, but he was early and he thought he would walk past the Gregory School to say hello.

As he passed Harriet Welsch's house on the corner of Eighty-seventh and East End, he saw her coming out the front door.

"Hey, Harriet!" he yelled.

"Hey, Sport!" she shouted, and ran down the steps. "What are you doing? Have you lost your mind? They won't let boys in this year."

"I know it." Sport laughed. "My school's down at Seventy-eighth. I just walked this way."

They fell into step together. Harriet looked him over.

"That's some suit you've got," she said finally.

"Thanks," said Sport and felt proud.

"I wish you were coming to school this year," said Harriet quietly. Sport looked at her. Harriet usually never said things like that. Maybe she was changing.

"Yeah. I wish I was, too. What's new? You away for the summer?"

"Yeah. Wow, did a lot happen, too. That Beth Ellen is something."

"Was she out there too?"

"Yeah. Crazy, mad thing she is. What's new with you?"

"Well, my father's getting married," said Sport.

"WHAT???" Harriet stopped and stared at him. "You're kidding!"

"No." Sport laughed. "It's true."

Harriet opened the notebook she always carried with her and wrote down this piece of information.

"Not that Zen Buddhist . . ." said Harriet, closing her notebook and looking at him, ". . . who turned out to be a belly dancer?"

"No," said Sport, and laughed at the memory of Kiki, the belly dancer. "This one's nice," he said.

"I've heard that before," said Harriet.

"No, she really is, honest," said Sport. "Want to come to the wedding?"

"SURE!!" said Harriet. She opened her notebook and wrote again. "When is it?"

"Next Friday," said Sport. "Come to the reception afterward at the house, after school."

"Sure!" said Harriet, slamming her notebook.

As they crossed Eighty-sixth Street, Harriet said, "Hey, there's Seymour and Harry."

Seymour and Harry were walking toward them. They stopped to let them catch up.

"Hey, creep," said Seymour, "we were coming to pick you up."

"Hey there, what are those rags?" said Harry,

pinching Sport's suit. "You look like Madison Avenue, man."

"Hi, Harriet," said Seymour.

Sport looked at Harry's tight pants very low on his hips, his high boots. I don't look that hip, he thought. I look like a banker. Seymour had on a plaid shirt, an old sweater, and blue jeans.

They all walked together down East End toward the Gregory School.

"Look at all the little snot girls going into school," said Harry, rolling an eye at Harriet, hoping to irritate her. He shot his long legs out in front of him when he walked, admiring his boots.

"Whew," said Seymour, "I could punch 'em all in the nose."

"Hey, there's Janie," said Sport, and yelled at her.

"Hey, Janie," said Harriet.

Janie was just going into school. She looked them over, gave a terrible grin, and walked inside without saying anything.

"What's eating her?" asked Sport.

"She hates boys this year. She's going through something. Can't stand the sight of them," Harriet said, writing furiously in her notebook.

"Who needs her?" said Harry.

"I could punch her right in the nose," said Seymour.

"Hi, Sport," said a funny little voice.

Looking around, Sport said, "Hi, Beth Ellen."

"Hi, Beth," said Harriet, not looking up from her notebook. The three boys stood looking alternately at Beth Ellen and at the sidewalk.

"How was your summer?" said Beth Ellen politely to Sport.

"Huh? Swell," said Sport.

"Come on," said Harriet suddenly to Beth Ellen and pushed her into school.

Beth Ellen looked back shyly and waved at Sport. All three boys waved back. They started off again down East End.

"Now there's a chick," said Harry. "A chick and a half."

"Yeah," said Seymour.

"She's something else," said Harry.

"Yeah," said Seymour. "Whynchu introduce us?" he said to Sport. "I coulda punched you right in the nose."

"Yeah," said Harry. "There we are standing there."

"Huh?" said Sport. "Oh, I didn't think of it."

Seymour gave him a push. "Such a punch I'll give you," he said, laughing.

Sport pushed him back. They all began punching and pushing and then they started to race each other to school. Harry won because his legs were longer. Sport was next and then Seymour, who was inclined to be a little fat and puffed a lot when he ran.

They slowed down. Sport looked up at the building. It looked like a prison. Seymour saw him looking at the school and said, "It's not bad. You oughta be glad it ain't the nuns. One year I was with the nuns. Wow. You turn around wrong, they punch you in the nose."

A small brown Puerto Rican boy came up to them and said, "Hey, Seymour, Harry, how're they doing?"

"Big, man, big," said Harry, laughing.

"How's it?" said Seymour, laughing.

Sport wondered what they were laughing at. He decided they liked to talk this way because it didn't make any sense. The boy stared at him. He stared back.

"How's the pickle-grabber? Hey, Chi-chi, how's the pickle-grabber?" asked Harry, laughing harder than ever.

"I'll punch her right in the nose," said Seymour, and the boy named Chi-chi laughed.

"She ain't getting it today," he said. "Yesterday she caught me by surprise."

Sport rubbed his new shoe on the sidewalk.

Chi-chi nodded toward him and said to Harry, "Who's the account executive?"

Harry laughed. "This is my friend Sport. He's

all right. He can't help it his ol' lady got him square clothes."

"Yeah," said Seymour. "This is Chi-chi, Sport."

Sport nodded. Chi-chi nodded. They both looked off up York Avenue.

"What's a pickle-grabber?" Sport asked Harry.

"Ah, this dumb girl. Every time she sees somebody's got a pickle in their lunch bag, she steals it. She's pickle-happy."

"Yeah. Next time she does it to me, I'm gonna punch her right in the nose," said Seymour with satisfaction.

"If you punched everybody in the nose you said you would," said Chi-chi, slowly smiling, "we wouldn't be able to walk for the bodies."

Sport and Harry laughed. Harry stuck his hands in his belt, pushed it even lower on his hips, and stomped his boots. Some girls at the door were looking at him.

"You shut up," said Seymour, "or I'll punch you right in the nose."

"Man, he's a broken record," said Chi-chi.

Seymour took a dive for Chi-chi, but Chi-chi ducked and Seymour went flying past.

"You gotta be quicker than that to get Chi-chi," said Harry.

Seymour gritted his teeth and said nothing.

"He has to dodge all those dames at the Plaza. Ain't nothing faster than Chi-chi when one of them's after him. I saw him take a curve in one of them halls at eighty miles an hour."

"And with a tray," said Chi-chi, laughing.

"You work at the Plaza?" asked Sport.

"Yeah," said Chi-chi, turning beautiful brown eyes on Sport. "I'm a busboy there after school and on weekends."

Seymour seemed to have forgotten his anger. "You make a lotta loot, don't you?" he asked.

"Yeah, 'specially off room service." He had a slow, soft way of talking. "Gotta be fast though. Some of them ol' ladies gets mighty lonely."

Harry laughed. A bell rang. Everyone turned toward the door. Sport felt his stomach drop. Harry and Seymour moved ahead. Sport went slowly. Chi-chi dropped back and said to him, "You have the first class with me. The teacher's a goon, but not mean. Stick next to me. We'll get seats together."

Sport felt grateful. They were all crushed in the doorway as the whole school seemed to arrive at once and pushed to get through the door.

Chapter 13

Sport found the new school much easier than the old one. He seemed to be having, in the seventh grade, the same things he had had in the sixth grade at the Gregory School. More than once during the week that followed, he was glad that he didn't have a lot of homework to do because his father and Kate were in such a flutter about the wedding that he wouldn't have been able to do it anyway. Sport was in a flutter about what the wedding was going to cost.

"Stop worrying," said his father.

"But you didn't even give me your royalty check to deposit," said Sport.

"I don't know how to break this to you, son," said Mr. Rocque, laughing and winking at Kate, "but you're fired."

"What does that mean?" asked Sport.

"Kate is going to manage all the money in this

household from now on." Mr. Rocque looked proudly at Kate. "She's very good at it."

"Yeah?" said Sport. Maybe she is, maybe she isn't, he thought. Anybody would be better than you. "But is there enough for all these plans you're making?" asked Sport. He had listened in horror for four days to plans for vintage champagne, kegs of beer, cases of whiskey, lavish buffets.

"No," said Kate. "We're not going to have all that. We decided last night. There's no reason for all that. My friends won't expect it and neither will Matthew's. We're going to have a keg of beer and a lot of marvelous sandwiches, an enormous loaf of pumpernickel, and lots of cold cuts. Everybody can make whatever they want."

Sport thought of his father's friends. They had always looked like a grubby lot to him.

"They'll be glad to get it," said Mr. Rocque. "I know for sure the last time Pete Rastoff ate was on Thursday at that exhibit that crazy rich wig gave. He called me up and described it to me. They had caviar and cold lobster. Pete called up all his friends and in three minutes the whole table was empty."

"She sell any paintings?" asked Kate.

"Of course not. Shouldn't have either; they were terrible."

"Don't you think you better feed him again before he's best man?" asked Sport.

"He might just keel over," said Kate.

"Pete? No, he'll do everything just right because he'll know he'll eat afterward."

"Did you decide where you're going after the wedding?" asked Sport.

"Out to Long Island," said Mr. Rocque.

"Out where Harriet goes for the summer? Water Mill?" asked Sport. He had visited Harriet for a weekend every summer.

"Out that way, but not so far. Closer to the city. Place called Quogue."

"Frog?" said Sport.

"Quogue, Q," said Kate. She laughed. "I am going back to my own apartment," said Kate. "I've got a million things to do before tomorrow." She leaned over and kissed the top of Mr. Rocque's head. She put on her coat. "Now, have we got all the plans straight?" she asked, looking at them both.

"We should by now," said Mr. Rocque. "We've talked about it enough."

"Okay. Let's just go over it once more," said Kate. "Sport, what do you do?"

"I get him up in time and make sure he gets on the right clothes."

"Right."

"Then I call Pete to make sure he's up. Then Pete picks him up."

"Right."

"Then what?" said Kate to Mr. Rocque.

"I forget."

"You pick me up, you big dope," said Kate, swinging her purse at him. "Who're you gonna marry, Pete?"

"Oh, yeah," said Mr. Rocque, smiling and rubbing his head. "We pick you up, then we pick up Marion, and then we go get married." He looked proudly at Kate.

"Ask him in the morning if he remembers, okay, Sport?" said Kate.

"Okay," said Sport. "Who's Marion?"

"My friend," said Kate. "You'll like her. Now, Sport, what do you do while we're gone?"

"Answer the door for the men from the delicatessen. Help them set up the food and put the glasses out and ice. Then answer the door for the guests."

"Right. In your pajamas?"

"Oh, yeah, I get dressed first, in my best suit."

"Right," said Kate. "And not the funeral one either. And here, here's a present for you, I almost forgot." She opened her purse and pulled out something wrapped in tissue paper. Sport opened it up.

"Hey, neat," he said and pulled out a red tie with white polka dots all over it. It looked like one of Harry's ties. "Great," he said to Kate. "Thanks."

"Wear that with your gray suit and a blue shirt and nobody will be able to resist you," said Kate.

"I'm going now. If anybody forgets what they have to do, just call."

Mr. Rocque got up and went out into the hall with her a minute. Sport put his tie in his room. "Hey," he yelled, running to the door. "I forgot to tell you. I invited Harriet. Is that okay?"

"Sure," said Mr. Rocque.

"Ask some more friends, if you like, Sport," said Kate, smiling. "There'll be plenty of Cokes and things. Anyway, you'll be happier."

"Thanks," said Sport wildly and ran inside to the phone to call up Seymour, Harry, and Chi-chi.

His father was reading the paper when he came back into the room.

"They're all coming," said Sport.

"Good," said his father, looking over the paper. "You look like you wish you hadn't asked them."

Sport shook his head. He looked at his sneakers. "Dad?"

"Yes?"

"I can't go there for the week."

"Come on, Sport. We've been all through this."

"Why don't you stay home? Even Long Island's going to cost something. I don't think we can afford it."

"Sport . . ." His father put down the paper. ". . . you don't seem to understand. You've inherited a lot of money."

"I understand, but I don't see any of it, and with Kate gonna live here and all, we need more money, Dad."

Mr. Rocque laughed. "We haven't seen any yet, it's true, and the estate will take a long time to settle, but Wilton said they'd be able to start paying some of the income right away. The bank does that. He told me to call him when I got back from the Island and tell him how much we need to live on."

"What are you gonna tell him?"

"I don't know yet. I thought I'd talk to Kate about it."

Sport felt left out. "Why don't you talk to me about it? I know how much we live on."

"What we live on now doesn't have anything to do with it, because Wilton said we should get another apartment. Also . . . I haven't brought this up before . . . but your mother wants you put in another school."

"What for? What's wrong with this one?"

"Nothing. I'm . . . we're discussing it. It hasn't been decided yet."

Sport got up and went into his room and slammed the door. He sat down on the bed. The whole blanking thing is a mess, he thought savagely, grinding his teeth. I just get to the point where I'm in the new school and . . .

"Sport, come on. I'm getting married in the

morning. I'm scared to death." His father was outside the door.

Sport opened the door.

"Come on, be a good old thing," said his father.
"I'm a wreck tonight."

"Okay," said Sport.

"You want to talk about it some time?"

"No."

"Good," said his father, obviously relieved. "Get
a good night's sleep."

"Sure."

His father turned away. Sport shut the door,
took off his clothes, and got into bed. "Something
is all wrong, something is one big blanking mess,"
he said over and over until he fell asleep.

Chapter 14

The next morning, Sport woke up terribly early. He got out of bed, looked at the clock, and saw that it was six thirty. He got back into bed and then remembered that it was the day of his father's wedding.

He huddled under the sheets to get warm. Everything will be different after today, he thought pleasantly, and then he remembered that everything was a blanking mess, that he had to spend a whole week with his mother, that he might have to go to a new school.

After a minute he thought he'd better get up and make the coffee. If he didn't get his father up by nine, he would never be able to leave the house by twelve. His father took hours to wake up, and two pots of coffee.

He got up and went into the kitchen. He noticed as he had before how clean everything had gotten since Kate came. He got out the coffee-pot. There was a piece of paper inside. He opened it up and read:

> *Dear Sport,*
>
> *Let's hope this is the last pot of coffee you'll ever have to make.*
>
> *I love you,*
> *Kate*

Sport smiled. It made him feel good. He made the coffee and went back to his room. He put on some jeans and his sweater, then went to his desk. He opened a drawer with a key. Taking out some large fat books, he put them on top of the desk. He ran his hand over the tops of them as though he were patting a puppy.

Next he went to the bottom drawer of his bureau and took out a small paper bag. Out of this he took out a small spool of white ribbon.

He went over to his desk and tied all of the fat books with the white ribbon. He stood back and looked at it. The bow looked kind of lopsided. He wrote a card and attached this to the ribbon with Scotch tape. Then he took the whole thing and hid it in the drawer that locked.

The coffee was perking as he came into the

kitchen. He turned it down and went to wake up his father. He didn't knock on the door but just went in.

His father was spread all over the bed; one long pajamaed leg was completely out of the bed with the foot stuck in the wastebasket. He lay on his back and his mouth was open.

Sport said, "Dad?"

"Gruuumph."

"Dad? It's morning,"

"What?" Mr. Rocque looked down. "Oh. Oh, yeah," he said abstractedly and climbed off the bed. He sat down and picked up a sock. "Coffee ready?" he said through a yawn.

"Yeah. You're getting married, remember?"

"What?" yawned his father. And then he heard him. "Oh, my God," he said loudly and jumped up. "What time is it?"

Sport laughed. "You got time. Take it easy. The coffee's ready. Come on and drink it."

Mr. Rocque looked sheepish. "Oh? Okay," he said dreamily, and having put on two different-colored socks, he weaved into the kitchen.

Sport took out the milk and poured himself a glass. He drank it looking at his father over the rim. I'll be glad, he thought, I'll be glad when Kate lives here all the time. I won't have to make the coffee, or clean the rooms, or keep the books, or anything.

Sport went back to work, and had the vacuuming done by the time his father finished a second pot of coffee. "You better take your shower now," he reminded him.

His father jumped up and, without looking right or left, tore into the bathroom.

Sport watched him and shook his head. "He doesn't know whether he's coming or going," he said to the empty room. "A regular dingbat," he added, using a word Chi-chi used to describe the ladies of the Plaza who were crazy.

He started in to clean the kitchen. After he had been scrubbing about ten minutes, he heard his father tear out of the shower. He gave an agonized yell from his bedroom. "Sport!"

Sport went down the hall, turned off the shower, and went into his father's room. Mr. Rocque stood in the middle of his room staring in consternation at a white shirt he held in his hands.

"No buttons," he whispered frantically to Sport. He looked as though he would cry.

"Never mind," said Sport, going to the bottom drawer of the bureau.

"Never mind?" squeaked Mr. Rocque.

Sport took out two new white shirts and a pile of new underwear. "Kate bought these for you. She thought this might happen. She told me not to tell you until this morning."

"Oh," said Mr. Rocque helplessly.

"She bought two because she said you might spill something on one."

"I have spilled something on the tie I thought I would wear."

"She bought a tie, too," said Sport calmly and handed it to him.

"What an angel she is," said Mr. Rocque sappily.

"Get dressed," said Sport. He went back to the kitchen. "She's sure getting some prize of a husband," he said to himself. "A regular dingbat."

After a while Sport went in and called Pete Rastoff who was, surprisingly, awake. "I even ate something," he said happily.

Mr. Rocque was finally ready. He surveyed himself proudly in the mirror. Sport looked him over. Everything looked just right, the handkerchief, the tie. "Dad!" he screamed. "You forgot to shave!"

"Oh, drat," said Mr. Rocque. Sport helped him off with his jacket and his shirt. He rushed in and shaved. He rushed back out again and Sport helped him put his shirt and jacket back on.

"Now what?" said Mr. Rocque, looking at himself nervously in the mirror.

"Now you get married," said Sport. He brushed him off and shoved him toward the door. "Pete's going to be right downstairs," he said, opening the door.

"How do you know?" asked Mr. Rocque vaguely.

The doorbell rang. "There he is," said Sport. "Now get on."

Mr. Rocque went obediently down the steps.

"Whew," said Sport after he had listened to hear if Mr. Rocque went out the front door. "So far, so good."

At two o'clock the delicatessen men arrived. They brought a folding table, set it up, filled it to overflowing with plates of food, tapped the keg of beer, and set up the bar.

At two thirty the guests started arriving. Sport answered the door, the man behind the bar gave them glasses of beer, and the man behind the table gave them food. The room was soon full.

Seymour, Harry, and Chi-chi arrived after school.

"Geez," said Seymour.

"Looka the food," said Harry.

"Hey, can we have a beer?" asked Seymour.

"No," said the man behind the bar, "here." He handed them Cokes. They started eating enormous plates of food.

"Hey, Sport," said Harry, "you look sharp."

Sport grinned.

"Whyncha eat?" asked Seymour.

"He's got the dingbats," said Chi-chi.

"What?" said Harry, leaning around a man with a beard coming back for his fourth pastrami sandwich.

"Nerves," said Chi-chi. "Not every day your old man gets married, right?"

"Right," said Sport. He tried to sound stalwart, but it came out a croak.

Harriet was at the door. She was all dressed up. Sport led her into the room and over to the table.

The boys all had their mouths full, but they nodded.

"Hey," said Chi-chi, "you look amazing, what?" He was trying to sound British but it came out vaguely Chinese.

Sport looked at Harriet. He realized she didn't even look like the same girl they'd seen in front of the school.

"Thank you," said Harriet to Chi-chi, whose large eyes opened wider.

"Want some food?" said Harry, holding out a plate to her.

"Thanks very much," said Harriet.

"Here," said Seymour, "here's a Coke."

What's the matter with these guys? thought Sport. They're all turning into dingbats. He went over to refill a glass of beer for a lady poet with three names. She was sitting next to a lady painter with her mouth full who grabbed Sport's arm and said, "Who is that lovely dark little boy with the big eyes?"

"You mean Chi-chi?" said Sport.

"Yes. Lovely. I'd like to have him pose for me."

Sport shrugged and went over to Chi-chi and told him.

"Ho-ho," said Seymour, overhearing, "better get your track shoes out, Chi-chi."

"What was that?" said Harriet. "What happened? I didn't hear. What happened?"

Chi-chi said, "Just a dumb dingbat."

"What?" said Harriet. "What is that? What happened?"

She might have kept this up indefinitely but for the fact that the door opened and in came Kate and Mr. Rocque. They both looked strangely beautiful, standing there in the doorway, all smiles, their friends jumping up all around them and running to kiss them, shake their hands, scream congratulations.

Mr. Rocque saw Sport and picked him right up off the ground. Sport felt like an idiot so he struggled to get down. Kate leaned over to him and kissed him. Pete Rastoff came in and rushed at the food like he was trying to put out a fire. Marion Sommers shook hands with Sport. Everyone started yelling and talking at once. Sport worked his way back to the other kids. They were all staring at Kate.

"Wow!" said Harry.

"Now there's a dame," said Seymour.

"She's beautiful," said Harriet.

"Whooee," said Chi-chi. "Hey, you're some lucky guy, Sport."

"Yeah," said Harriet. "She came and said hello to us already. She's nice."

"Yeah," said Sport, and grabbing a plate, he began piling things on it. He started to eat like he'd never eaten before. He looked over and saw Pete Rastoff still gobbling. All the kids continued eating the entire time they were there.

"I've had four Cokes and eight tomato sandwiches," said Harriet, sitting down suddenly as though her stomach had pushed her over.

"How can you eat tomato sandwiches when there's all this good food?" said Sport, his mouth full of pastrami.

"I like tomato sandwiches," said Harriet with dignity. "I did put a piece of ham on one of them, but it ruined the taste."

"Whyncha bring that friend of yours?" said Seymour, sidling up to Harriet. "What's her name? Uh, Beth something?"

"I didn't know she was invited," said Harriet.

"You could've," said Sport. "I didn't think."

"I'll give you a punch," said Seymour.

A man in the back of the room started playing a guitar. A guy with a beard jumped up and started dancing very fast.

"He looks like he got an itch," said Harry.

From the small white purse she was carrying, Harriet pulled an even smaller notebook. She wrote furiously in it, looking up at the party every now and then.

"Whatsamatter with her?" whispered Harry to Sport. "She work for the FBI?"

Sport laughed. "Maybe she can't remember anything 'less she writes it down," said Chi-chi.

Harriet paid no attention to them. She kept on writing away. Everyone in the room was dancing suddenly. Chi-chi started doing a wild dance. Seymour stomped his feet a little, but he wasn't very good.

"I can't dance," said Harry.

"I can't either," said Sport, thinking, I never even tried.

Harriet looked up from her notebook. "Janie and I have to go to dancing school," she said morosely.

"Whew," said Harry. "What are you learning? The hustle?"

"The waltz," said Harriet sadly.

The party got noisier and noisier. Kate came over to them once and asked them if they were getting everything they wanted. Sport tried to say yes but burped instead, which made her laugh.

"Hey, Kate," he said as she started to walk away.

"Yes, darling?" she said, coming back to him.

"You got a minute?"

"Sure, what?"

"Come with me," said Sport, and taking her hand, he pushed through the crowd to his room. They went inside, and he closed the door.

"What is it, darling?" said Kate.

"I got a present for you," said Sport as he unlocked the big drawer of his desk. "Here," he said, turning around and handing her the books tied with white ribbon. The card on top said FOR KATE.

"What's this?" she asked softly. "Oh . . . ledgers?"

"They're my books that I keep the money in. I thought since you're gonna keep the money now, maybe you . . ." He wound down. It seemed silly now, the whole idea of giving them to her.

"Oh, my darling." Kate grabbed him in a big hug, kissing the top of his head. "What a wonderful thing to do." There were tears in her voice and in her eyes. "It's all going to be so great," she whispered, holding him close, then pulling back and drying her eyes with her hand.

"Here," said Sport and handed her his handkerchief.

"Thank you. My, what a gentleman," she said, laughing. "Oh, dear, I may cry again."

Sport kicked the floor with his shoe. "You could leave 'em in here," he said, gesturing to the books.

"What? Oh, yes, I guess I can't wander around

the party with ledgers, can I?" She put them on the bed. "Although I'd like to. It's the nicest present I ever got." She turned back to him. "Thanks," she said simply in a way that didn't embarrass Sport at all.

BOOK THREE

Chapter 15

Egbert held the door open. Sport got into the long car. Mr. Wilton said, "Hello. That isn't a very big bag for a week's stay."

"It's got all the clothes I own," said Sport, watching Egbert put the old overnight case of his father's in the front seat. He felt terrible. His father and Kate were upstairs. They were all packed and had only been waiting until Mr. Wilton came for him. They would leave for the beach now. He wouldn't see them for a week.

"Are those your schoolbooks?" asked Mr. Wilton as the car pulled away from the curb. He pointed to the books Sport carried.

"Yes, and one my father gave me to read," said Sport.

"Oh, let's see," said Mr. Wilton and reached for the book. Sport handed it to him thinking, I don't like that. It's none of his fat business.

Mr. Wilton laughed when he saw the title.

Sport was furious. The book was about the stock market. He was interested in the stock market and his father had bought the book for him. He had said, "Now that you'll have some money you may want to learn how to invest it." Sport had been delighted. What right had this man to laugh at it? He looked out the window and gritted his teeth.

"That's a good book," said Mr. Wilton. "I've read it. There's some very sound advice in it. Of course you won't have to worry about that sort of thing for a while. Your money will all be invested for you until you're thirty-five."

"I'm not worried about anything," said Sport sullenly. He took the book back, put it with his other books, and looked out the window.

"I'm glad," said Mr. Wilton. "I wish I could say the same."

There was a closed-in silence as the car slid along the street. Why do grown-ups all ask for sympathy? thought Sport. Kids don't ever do that. What the friz does he have to be worried about? Here I am having to spend a week with a dingbat of a mother.

After about ten blocks Mr. Wilton shifted in his seat as though he were uncomfortable and said, "What I mean is, I'm worried because you're spending this week with your mother."

Why should you be worried? thought Sport, but he said nothing.

"Your mother . . ." began Mr. Wilton, but didn't finish the sentence. "I don't know what she's going to do with you."

What am I going to do with her? is the question, thought Sport.

"She seems to be out all the time," said Mr. Wilton, as though he were thinking aloud.

There was another silence, and then he said quite definitely, "This is what I'm trying to say to you, Simon. If you are unhappy this week, I want you to call me." He took out a piece of paper and jotted down something. "Here is my phone number at the office and the hours I am there. Here is the number of my home. You may call me at any hour. I would like to know if something goes wrong."

It's all wrong right now, thought Sport. It's wrong now and it will stay wrong. He kept trying to remember what his father had said. That Charlotte would get sick of having a kid around. She makes me sick, thought Sport, she makes me sick right now.

"Will you do that?" asked Mr. Wilton as Sport took the piece of paper.

"Yes," he said, thinking, I'd be scared to call you. If she caught me, what would she do?

The car pulled up in front of the house.

* * *

That night when Sport went to bed, he had never been so exhausted in his life. His mother had started right out by taking him to P. J. Clarke's for brunch. He had gotten through a hamburger and a Coke, then sat for three hours while friend after friend after friend had joined her for Bloody Marys. There were always at least five people at the table, but not always the same people. They would come, drink, and leave, only to be replaced by more. Sport wandered away from the table several times and was not even missed.

He was just thinking that it would be very easy to leave and take a cab to his apartment, when his mother noticed him. He went through another round of introductions. I'm some kind of midget escort, he thought as he bounced up again because some old lady came to the table.

When finally there was no one else to greet, his mother said, "We're going to Saks now." She seemed to say it to the air, but then remembered he was there and added brightly, "Won't that be fun?"

"A barrel of monkeys," said Sport, but the sound of his voice had made her deaf again.

They made the sidewalk with Charlotte only staggering once as they went through the bar. The bright September sun hit their faces and blinded Sport as he took up his position near the curb to hail a cab.

At Saks he sat on a spindly chair while she tried on clothes.

She hailed another cab and they went to another store. At the end of the day they had gone to four stores and had hailed six cabs. I could get a job as a doorman easy now, he thought, as they got out of the last one in front of the house.

"The next time, I'll give you the money and you can pay for the cabs," said Charlotte as they were going up the steps.

"Whoopee," said Sport sourly.

"You must learn to be a gentleman," she said briskly.

When I'm with a lady I am, thought Sport. Kate's face came into his mind and made him gulp. He had no time for feelings, however, because when they went in the front door, they discovered that the house was full of people.

"Oh, Lord, I forgot," said Charlotte. "Carrie is having people."

Carrie's party turned out to be a simple little affair of two hundred people. Charlotte rushed Sport past the drawing room with a hissed, "Get upstairs. We must change."

He went into his room. He closed the door and walked around looking at everything. The room looked like a mausoleum. The furnishings were enormous. Sport felt like he had to crawl up on everything he sat on. There was even a little step stool to crawl into the bed.

The lowest thing in the room was a chaise in the corner next to a window. He went and sat down.

He stared around the room. It looks like something in a horror movie, he thought. Someone with a terrible face will step out of that armoire any minute. I'll be frizzled if I'll go down to any blanking party.

He contented himself with pretending that he was talking to Seymour. Blanking woman took me to so many blanking stores, I'm blanked out. He could almost hear Seymour saying, "Give her a punch in the nose."

There was a knock on the door. Sport said nothing. The door opened anyway and a small man who looked like a Filipino stuck his head in.

"I am to help you dress, no?" he said in a light voice.

"No," said Sport.

"Dress for party. Miss Vane say I help you dress for party," he said cheerily and bounced into the room.

"I'm not going to the party," said Sport.

The man was at the armoire taking out Sport's black suit. "Very nice," he said. "Dress very nice for party."

What a jingle bell, thought Sport. He hoped a corpse would fall out of the armoire onto the man, but nothing happened. The suit was laid on the bed. The little man rushed to the chest and took out a shirt, tie, underwear.

"Now," he said gleefully, and reached for the buttons on Sport's jacket.

"I dress myself," Sport shouted.

"Very nice," said the little man, and when Sport unbuttoned his jacket he helped him take it off.

I give up, thought Sport, and standing still, he allowed himself to be undressed and then dressed. If Harry or Seymour or Chi-chi could see me now, he thought, I would be laughed out of Manhattan.

The little man brushed him off thoroughly and then stood back to look at the results. "Very nice," he said.

He propelled Sport toward the door, keeping a lovely smile on his face and only gently pushing. Nevertheless, Sport found himself downstairs in record time.

The cocktail party was in full swing. Sport edged his way into the crowd, so short that he wasn't noticed.

"Rather soon after the death to have such a *large* party, don't you think?" said a lady with a martini to a man with an old-fashioned.

"Typical of Charlotte and Carrie," said the man. "It's a wonder they noticed he's dead."

The martini lady went into a gale of laughter

that made Sport's ears hurt. He edged past another group, staying as close as he could to the wall and not looking at anyone so he wouldn't be noticed.

What will I do with myself? he thought frantically. I can't just stand around this room all night. He thought of calling Seymour on the phone and screaming, "Help! I'm trapped in a Chinese cocktail party." Seymour would laugh, but he wouldn't be much help. He thought of what Mr. Wilton had said about calling him, but he didn't know what he would say. Nobody was doing anything *wrong* to him. This was just the way his mother lived.

"There you are, little darling," His mother stretched a long arm his way and pulled him into the group. "Here he is, my little man," she said loudly and pushed him around to show him off. She turned him to the right and left as though she wanted them to see all sides of him. I feel like I'm in the Westminster Dog Show, thought Sport. Maybe I should bark.

"Hello there," said a woman.

"Hello, young fellow," said a man.

"My," said a woman, somewhat ambiguously.

"How old are you, dear?" said another woman, shouting above the noise.

"Forty-seven," said Sport.

"You're tall for your age," trilled the woman, not having heard a thing.

"Would you like some cranberry juice?" asked Charlotte.

"Cranberry juice!" shouted Sport. Oh, this is ridiculous. Wait'll I tell Seymour, he thought, muttering "cranberry juice" under his breath.

"Hello there, sonny," said a strange-looking giant of a man. He leaned over to Sport. Sport almost fell down from his breath. He blew a great puff of pipe smoke into Sport's face. "Come over here and talk to me awhile," said the man. He motioned toward a love seat, and there was nothing to do but follow him. "I have a son around your age," said the man, settling down on the seat and blowing more smoke.

Sport squeezed into the tiny place left for him and coughed from the smoke.

"He and I are having a little problem," said the man.

"I thought I might discuss it with an unbiased person of his own age." Another whirl of smoke caught Sport right in the eye. Trying to look biased, he nodded through the smoke.

"You see, I think it's time he went off to school, but he wants to remain in New York."

"Why don't you just pack him up and send him off?" asked Sport, wincing a little because a woman had just ground her high heel into his foot.

"Ha-ha," said the man, releasing a really foul stream of breath. Sport gasped. He pretended to reach up and scratch his face, but in reality he held his nose.

"Oh, I don't want to do that," continued the man. "I want him to like the idea." He looked at Sport and arched his eyebrows.

"He doesn't," said Sport and held his nose again in case the man laughed. He seemed to make a habit of laughing when nothing was funny.

"Well, heh-heh, I thought perhaps you might have some ideas about what might get him to like it." The man gave Sport a pitiful look.

"Maybe you should stop bugging him, you smelly old jingle bell," said Sport loudly and jumped up and ran before the man could hit him. Across the room, he peered through the crook of an elbow and saw the man heave himself to his feet and lumber over to someone else.

Aw, why'd I do that? thought Sport. He probably just doesn't have anybody to talk to either. He put his hands in his pockets and moved around the room as though he had someplace to go. If I keep moving no one will say anything to me, he reasoned. It was hard though, because he had to avoid both Charlotte and the smelly old man now. He went in small circles, staring at nothing. I'm hungry, he thought with irritation. I wonder when they have dinner in this joint.

A hand came down on the back of his neck. It gripped like a steel collar. "How dare you be insulting to Hayworth Brown, Junior," Charlotte spit in his ear.

When he looked up at her, she was smiling over his head. She kept on smiling in a vacant way as she continued: "He's one of the richest men in town. He's the son of Hayworth Dalton Brown," she said with a swift intake of breath.

Sport tried to pull away, but her hand was like a bear trap. "He passed it off as a joke, of course, but I could see that he wasn't amused, and I am not one bit amused. You're going to bed without your supper, young man."

Sport looked up at her in horror.

"Oh, yes. You will learn your manners right now. Up the stairs," she said, still smiling vacantly over his shoulder. She gave him a push.

He pushed his way out through the people and went up the steps to his room.

When he got there, he got out the money his father had given him and put it in his pocket. He put all his clothes back in the old suitcase and rammed his books in on top of them.

He opened the door to his room. A maid whipped by. Then the hall was empty. He tiptoed out and around a corner looking for a back staircase. He found one and started sneaking down. As he was about to round a corner he heard voices.

"We can't be out of anchovies."

"We are."

"Hop to Gristede's right now then, miss. Be quick about it."

Silence. Sport went around the corner and found himself in a butler's pantry off the kitchen. He sneaked through this and found a hall which led to a side door. He jumped out the door and ran for his life up the street. He found a cab quickly and, jumping in, he gave the driver his address.

"Moving?" said the driver.

"What? Yeah," said Sport.

"Wouldn't be running away, would you?" asked the driver, craning around to get a look at him.

"What? No. Going to my grandmother's," mumbled Sport.

"Oh? Got to be careful, you know. Police ask if we've seen some boy, you know how it is."

"Yeah," said Sport, wondering how it was.

The driver didn't say any more. They pulled up in front of his house and he got out and ran upstairs.

He didn't have the key. He had given his key to Kate in case Mr. Rocque lost his. What'll I do now? He remembered Mr. Collins, the landlord. He ran downstairs and rang his bell.

"What? Who is it?" bellowed Mr. Collins.

"I forgot my key," said Sport.

Mr. Collins opened the door. "Oh. Hi there, Mr. C.P.A."

"I forgot my key. Could I have the extra one?"

"What? Sure. Here you go," said Mr. Collins, reaching behind the door to a board he had with all the keys on it. "There you go."

"Thanks." Sport ran away before he could say any more to him.

"Nice suit you got there," yelled Mr. Collins up the steps. "Some party you folks gave last night," he shouted.

"Yeah," said Sport. He got the door open and went into the apartment. He set his suitcase down with a thump. "Whew!"

He looked around. The shades were all pulled down. He went around and pulled them up. He went into the kitchen and looked in the icebox. There were a lot of things left over from the party. He got them out and put them on the table. He opened a Coke and began to eat everything he could get his hands on, cramming it into his mouth.

Maybe I could find out where they are on Long Island and go there. No, he cautioned himself, I've heard that people like to be alone on their honeymoons. Maybe I could go to Seymour's.

He went in and called Seymour on the phone. No one answered. Mrs. O'Neil was in the store, so Seymour must be out. He thought about going over to the store, but instead he called Harry.

"Harry?"

"Yeah. Hi, Sport. I thought you were over to your mother's."

"I left. I ran away."

"Yeah? No friz?"

"Yeah. Listen, Harry, could you put me up there?"

"Geez. We only got the two beds, Sport. Me and my two brothers are in one and my mother and sister are in the other one. Tonight we even got my uncle on the couch."

"Oh."

"What happened?"

"Aaah, the blanking woman. She ran me all over town all day opening doors for her and putting her in cabs and things, then there's this blanking party with these blanking bores all over the place when we got home and she makes me go to it. Hey, Harry, some guy came up and dressed me!"

"You mean like a valet? Like the movies?" Harry shrieked.

"Yeah. Got the picture? He makes me go to this party so some lousy guy with bad breath starts bellyaching at me, so I call him a jingle bell. So the blanking woman sends me to bed with no dinner! I'm starving, and she sends me upstairs. So I left."

"Geez," said Harry, impressed. "What you gonna do now?"

"I don't know. I tried to get Seymour. If I sleep here, they'll come get me, I think."

"Seymour and his mother had to go to Jersey. Some uncle died, so they closed the store and went over there."

"Geez," said Sport.

"I wish I could put you up here. Hey, I could stay at your house and you stay here, then when they come to get you . . . Naw, that wouldn't work. They find me there, they put me in jail." Harry sounded worried. "I know what you do, Sport. See, you turn out all the lights and you pull the shades down like there's nobody there. Then when they ring the bell, you don't answer."

"Yeah," said Sport.

"That way they think nobody's there," said Harry. "You got enough food?"

"Sure, left over from the party."

"Oh, wow," said Harry, "I oughta come over there and eat."

"Come on, there's a lot."

"Naw, I ate already. I'll come in the morning."

"Okay."

"Take it easy, Sport. Hey, Sport, you wanta get rid of your old lady?"

"Whataya mean?" asked Sport nervously. He didn't want to bump anybody off.

"Just ask me over for tea!" said Harry and went off in a high cackle that tore through the phone.

"Crazy, man," said Sport.

"Okay, so long now," said Harry.

"So long," said Sport and hung up. He felt horribly alone as he put the phone down.

He turned off the lights and pulled down all the shades. He sat in the gloom on the couch until he began to fall asleep and then he went into his room and lay down on his bed.

Chapter 16

The next thing he knew, there was a lot of yelling, a light being turned on over his head, and Mr. Wilton standing looking down at him. It was Mr. Collins doing the yelling. He waddled in the door saying, "Don't like these goings on. How'm I to know his father's out of town? All I know, they had a party raise the roof last night on till three in the morning, crashing around, screaming . . ."

"Thank you for opening the door," said Mr. Wilton coldly. "I shall keep the key until his father returns."

"I need the key . . ." started Mr. Collins.

"If you need the key, you can place a call to me and you will have the key as quickly as it is humanly possible to get it to you." There was something about Mr. Wilton's voice that shut Mr. Collins up. He looked at Mr. Wilton with his eyes bugging as Mr. Wilton handed him his card.

"Yes," said Mr. Collins and left the room still squinting at the card.

"I suggest you get up," said Mr. Wilton.

Sport stood up.

"Comb your hair and wash your face," said Mr. Wilton.

Sport went into the bathroom. He looked at himself in the mirror. His eyes looked small and sleepy and helpless. He started to feel a terrible sadness. He washed his face and dried it with a towel that smelled like Kate. The smell made him remember what his father had said about Charlotte getting sick of having him around. "I'll make her sick," he said to himself in the mirror. He clenched his jaw, trying to look like Agent 007. "I'll make her pay to get rid of me," he growled at himself.

He flung the towel on the floor, thought of Kate, and leaned down to pick it up. He hung it neatly, went out into the living room, and marched to the front door.

"Where are you going?" asked Mr. Wilton, hurriedly rising from the couch.

"Back to prison, where else?" said Sport, and walked out the door.

He went down the steps. He heard Wilton behind him closing and locking the door. The next time I come back here, said Sport to himself, it'll be for good.

He climbed into the car before Egbert had time

to hop out and open the door. Mr. Wilton followed. They rode back to Charlotte's house without a word.

The party was still going on. Mr. Wilton led Sport through the side door and up to his room. Sport sat down on the chaise and folded his arms. Mr. Wilton put the still unopened suitcase on a chair, took out Sport's pajamas, and put them on the bed.

He pulled up another chair and sat down across from Sport. "Simon, I think we ought to have a talk."

Sport said nothing.

"Something seems to be bothering you," he continued. "What seems to be the trouble?"

There was no way to even begin to tell him, so Sport kept his mouth shut.

"You're not happy here?"

Silence.

"Are there things you want you're not getting?"

Yeah, my father and Kate, you jingle bell, thought Sport.

"If so, you must tell me. I want you to be able to trust me. I'm on your side.

"I know it's hard to make the adjustment right at first, but you cannot run away again. Your grandfather wanted, more than anything in the world, for you to be happy. He has arranged things in such a way that he thought would make you happy. I think the least you can do is to give it a fair trial."

Sport began to sink down somewhere inside himself. What is happening? he asked himself. Why has everybody gone crazy? What is this man talking about?

"We'll have a talk in the morning," said Wilton in a kind voice. He replaced the chair. "Get some sleep now." He smiled once quickly at the bed as though he found the pajamas amusing, and went out of the room. Sport heard a key turn in the lock.

I'm locked in, he thought wildly. He tried, unsuccessfully, to think what Agent 007 might do. He got up, undressed mechanically, and got into bed. There'll be a way, he thought as he fell asleep. There's always a way. I'll play it by ear and I'll find a way.

Chapter 17

The next morning there was a summit meeting after breakfast. Sport felt very much awake, eager to listen, but he showed nothing. He tried to look sleepy.

"I thought we should have a little discussion," said Wilton by way of opening the meeting.

"Too boring," said Charlotte. "It's simply bad behavior and should be punished." She was so furious that she wouldn't look at Sport.

"I think we are a little more enlightened these days, Charlotte," said Wilton mildly.

"Perhaps he is lonely," said Carrie.

"Ridiculous," said Charlotte. She stared hard at Sport. "You are not to run away again. Do you understand that?"

Sport laughed right in her face.

"You see?" said Charlotte. "He's been raised in a barn. I know Matthew. Matthew has never heard of good manners. The boy is a savage."

"Charlotte," said Wilton in a warning voice. "There is a reason the boy ran away. Why don't we ask him?"

"Perhaps he misses his little friends," whined Carrie.

"Well, if he thinks I'm going to fill up this house with a lot of nasty children, he's wrong," said Charlotte.

"Simon," said Wilton calmly. "I'd like you to tell us why you did what you did."

There was a silence. Charlotte snorted. Now's my chance, thought Sport. Taking his cue from Carrie, he said, "There aren't any other kids here."

"Carrie, you're such a fool," said Charlotte.

"No," said Wilton. "Perhaps Carrie was simply right. It's lonely with no one but grown-ups around. Is that right, Simon?"

"Yes," said Sport, attempting to look pitiful.

"There, you see," said Carrie triumphantly.

"I will not have it," said Charlotte. "A lot of dirty children from the streets tramping through here, breaking things."

"Now wait a minute," said Wilton calmly. "Simon went to a very good school. I'm sure the children from the Gregory School are very well behaved. They're nice children, aren't they, Simon?"

"Yes," said Sport.

"It's very simple," said Carrie. "We'll invite two or three over today for lunch."

"Fine," said Wilton. "How does that sound, Simon?"

"Fine," said Sport. Oh, goody, oh golly gee, is what I should say, he told himself and started laughing in his head. His face showed absolutely nothing.

"Fine," said Wilton. "Run along and call them up."

"Needless to say, I will go out to lunch," said Charlotte as Sport went through the door.

"Charlotte," said Wilton, "you are making a big mistake." His voice took on a courtroom sound. "I am warning you. If you want to keep this boy . . ." Sport had to close the door so he couldn't hear the rest.

He went to an upstairs phone where no one could hear him. He made three calls. During each call he gave long and involved instructions with many interjections of "Get what I mean?" and "Got it?"

Everybody got it.

At twelve thirty Charlotte was sitting, visibly unhappy, with Sport in the drawing room. The doorbell rang. Charlotte was unable to suppress a tiny groan.

His friends, who had arrived together, were ushered into the room.

Harriet came first, pushing ahead of the butler

in her eagerness to see everything. She was dressed in her best dress, her best coat, and, wonder of wonders, a leghorn hat which crashed against the doorsill and thereafter sat crooked upon her head.

Harry came next, dressed in the most important-looking suit Sport had ever seen. He looked like the Duke of Windsor, only brown. His slim boots were polished to a blinding glow, his tight, gray flannel suit was beautifully cut and fell gracefully back into place as he moved into the room.

Seymour looked as though he were going to be Bar Mitzvahed. His hair had been plastered wet into his head, his dark blue suit, though a bit tight across the chest, was newly cleaned and pressed. His shirt was gleaming white, his tie a cheerful red. He could have posed for the child of an Irish cop.

Charlotte was dutifully introduced to each in turn. She blinked at the word *Seymour*, but said nothing.

They all sat down around the coffee table. Each was well rehearsed and they began their scenes with Harriet taking off her hat. Out of her hat she took a notebook and a pen.

Chatting away nervously, Charlotte watched her out of the corner of her eye. For one terrible moment Sport thought he was going to have to feel sorry for her because she seemed more nervous than the kids, but her conversation was so inane that it destroyed any compassion he might have felt.

"You all attend the Gregory School?" she said in a strange, fluting voice, looking wonderingly at the knife crease in Harry's pants.

"Oh, yes," said Seymour in a completely unnatural voice.

"I say, that we do," said Harry in a British accent.

Harriet had started to write down everything furiously.

Charlotte flicked her eyes at Harriet, then looked away quickly. Harriet wrote that down, too.

"I hear that it's a very good school," said Charlotte vaguely as she watched Harriet.

"Quite," said Harry.

"I have, of course, been out of the country for so long . . ." said Charlotte.

"Of course," said Harry.

". . . but I'm told that only the best families . . ." Charlotte broke off because Harriet was leaning over almost in her face as she took down her words.

"Oh, ra-ther," said Harry.

Charlotte was plainly at a loss for words. She rang a small bell on the table. The butler appeared at the door almost instantly. "Tell Miss Carrie that our guests are here," she said in a clipped way that made Sport know she was desperate. "And bring me a martini. Oh, and bring the children something . . . cranberry juice."

"*Cranberry juice?*" said Harriet loudly.

The butler went away. Charlotte looked around desperately as though she would find something to say lying on the floor.

Harriet's pen stopped writing. She looked around curiously. Seymour coughed. Harry flicked imaginary dust from his sleeve.

"It's a beautiful day," said Seymour. He said it eagerly. It was plain that he was the oh-golly-gee lead in this play.

"Been rather muggy lately," said Harry.

"Yes, it has," said Charlotte, as though the weather were fascinating. "The weather has been dreadful. I was just saying the other day, I cannot remember such a long, dreadful stretch of bad weather."

What are they talking about? thought Sport. There haven't been anything but sunny days lately.

Carrie came in. Seymour, Harry, and Sport jumped to their feet.

"Oh, my, how nice," said Carrie, her eyes glazing over as they rested an undue length of time on Harry.

Sport introduced everyone.

"How do you do?" said Harriet, nodding briefly and resuming her writing.

"Pleased to meet you," said Seymour and looked eager.

"Enchanted," said Harry.

Carrie's eyebrows went up. She took the chair next to Sport, moving around Harry as though he were an iceberg.

"We were just talking about the children who attend the Gregory School," said Charlotte.

"Oh, yes," said Carrie. She turned to Harriet. "Your name is Welsh? I think I knew your grandfather," she said sweetly.

"Oh, yeah?" said Harriet. "Wasn't he funny?"

"Funny?" said Carrie.

"Yeah," said Harriet. "I mean, all that corn liquor and everything."

"Oh," said Carrie. "Perhaps I'm mistaken. I thought I knew most of the families who send their children to Gregory. My dear little daughter went there before she . . . passed away.

"She died?" asked Seymour eagerly.

"What of?" asked Harriet.

"Oh, dear," said Carrie, and looked away.

"Let's see," said Charlotte, trying to change the subject. She turned to Seymour. "What did you say your last name was . . . ah . . . Serge?"

"Seymour," corrected Seymour. "My last name is O'Neil."

"Curious," said Charlotte and then, "Thank you" to the butler who had brought the martini and large glasses of cranberry juice for the children. "I don't know any O'Neils at all."

Carrie had stopped snuffling into her handkerchief about her daughter and was staring hard at Harriet. Harriet went on writing.

"Do you have so much homework, child?" Carrie finally said to Harriet just as Charlotte, having had two large swallows of the martini, turned to Harry and said brightly, "And of course your father must be with the United Nations."

"I beg your pardon," said Harry.

"I say, your father must be one of the ambassadors, Indian perhaps, at the U.N.?" Charlotte seemed considerably more chipper. Carrie looked relieved at the idea.

"Do you mean, am I an Indian?" asked Harry in a clipped voice.

"Yes," said Charlotte. Carrie nodded her head.

"No, ma'am, I'm just plain American nigger," said Harry. Charlotte slopped her martini, she put it down so fast.

Carrie fainted dead away.

Seymour, Sport, and Harriet laughed.

Charlotte regained her voice. She stood up. "Simon, get these people out of here. I will not be talked to this way. And look what you've done to Carrie. Get something, do something."

Harriet threw a glass of cranberry juice in Carrie's face.

Charlotte screamed. "Out! Get out! All of you!"

Carrie looked like she'd been murdered now with all the juice running off her head.

Harry stood up. He bowed politely from the waist and said, "Thank you ever so much for a lovely lunch."

Seymour followed suit. "Gee, I had a swell time," he said, grinning over at Carrie.

Harriet put her notebook back in her hat and smashed the hat down on her head. She jumped up and said, "See ya, Sport." The three of them went out.

Charlotte rang the bell frantically. The butler appeared. "Watch those three on the way out," shouted Charlotte. "They'll steal the silver. Do something, call the doctor, Miss Carrie has fainted. Take this boy up to his room." The butler didn't know what to do first. He ran in three directions for a few seconds, then left the room.

Charlotte ran to the phone. Carrie began to rouse herself as Charlotte screamed into the phone. "Wilton, this was your idea! His little *friends*, as you call them, turn out to be one fat, hairy thing who looks forty, one black as pitch, and one schizophrenic who writes in a book the whole time! I told you before, Wilton, and now I know I'm right, this boy has to be removed from the influence of his father immediately."

"I'm bleeding to death," screamed Carrie.

"No, it's cranberry juice," said Sport.

". . . I want his custody immediately," said Charlotte. She wasn't shouting now. She spoke with a concentrated coldness of tone that made Sport shiver.

". . . I don't care what you have to do and I don't care how long it takes . . . I want his custody and I'm going to get it."

"You should be severely punished," said Carrie, leering at Sport through one cranberry-red eye. She got up and squished out of the room with as much dignity as she could muster.

Charlotte slammed the phone down. She stood still when she saw that Sport was still there. She pointed her finger at him.

"You're getting away from those people before you're completely ruined. Get upstairs to your room. This week you're going to learn what the word discipline means."

Sport stood up.

"Move," she shouted.

Sport went up to his room. He climbed up on the big bed and laughed. He laughed and laughed, remembering Charlotte's face as she listened to Harry. He kept on laughing even when he heard the key turn in the lock and knew he was locked in for good.

Chapter 18

During the next week things were so bad, Sport wondered if the laugh had been worth it. Instead of wanting to get rid of him, Charlotte seemed to want to keep him forever.

Egbert drove him to school every morning in the long black car. He tried to get Egbert to stop a block away from the school and let him out so the kids wouldn't see him, but Egbert just shook his head. When school let out, Egbert was right back again. Sport was taken back home, escorted to his room, and locked in. He got to be the smartest boy in class that week because there was nothing to do in that room but his homework. He began to be a little groggy about what day it was because they were all so much alike. He was unlocked, dressed for dinner by the Filipino, and led to the table. Once there, he had no appetite. Each meal was a long lesson in table manners. Food seemed totally unimportant next to remembering where to put the fingerbowl. He was led back upstairs again, undressed, and put into bed. The little man smiled the whole time as though it were all delightful.

The first day back at school he and Harry and Seymour had laughed a lot.

"Anytime you want the room cleared, just call," said Harry.

"Yeah," said Seymour. "For LEWD's first case I think we brought it off pretty good."

"Elementary, my dear Serge," said Harry.

After the first day, however, they just looked at him when he got into the black car. He watched them through the back window with envy as they walked off together to play ball.

Toward the end of the week Sport began to feel better. After all, he reasoned, my father will be home Saturday afternoon. They said they wanted to spend Sunday with me before they both had to go back to work. He sat dreaming through most of Friday. Friday night he was so excited, he couldn't go to sleep.

He wondered why no one had mentioned his father's return or his going home. They must remember my father is coming home Saturday, he thought nervously. He finally got to sleep. He thought he was dreaming when he saw Charlotte, fully dressed, leaning over his bed.

"Get up now," she said, not unkindly.

"What?" said Sport. "I don't have school today," he said groggily.

"Get up and put on your gray suit," she said shortly and left the room.

Maybe my father is here early, Sport thought happily and jumped out of bed. He hurried into his clothes, threw everything into the suitcase, and ran downstairs without brushing his teeth. Charlotte was waiting for him in the front hall. Without a word, she pushed him out the front door and into the waiting car.

Whew, said Sport to himself, it's over.

The car started off. Instead of turning uptown it turned downtown. Sport felt his heart start to jump. "Where's he going?" he asked loudly.

Charlotte said nothing.

"Where's he going?" Sport repeated frantically.

Charlotte still said nothing. Sport looked at her face. Her jaw was tense, her eyes cold and hard as she stared straight ahead at the back of Egbert's neck.

"Where're you taking me?" yelled Sport and grabbed at her fur coat.

"Take your hands off me," she said quietly. "And shut up." Her voice was a stiletto. Sport stared at her a minute, then looked out the window to see where they were going. They were on Fifth Avenue headed downtown. Egbert made a turn into Fifty-ninth Street and pulled up at the front door of the Plaza Hotel.

The doorman opened the door, and Charlotte got out. She motioned impatiently for Sport. He crawled out and followed her up the steps. She went around the Palm Court to the desk, said a few words to the man there, and handed the bellboy a key. She turned toward the elevator. Sport had just decided to run out the side door when she spotted him and pulled him to the elevator. She told the man the floor. The bellboy came with them and carried Sport's bag. He opened the door to a room, and they stepped inside. Charlotte tipped him and he left. Sport stood in the middle of the room, looking at his mother in wonder.

She turned around to him. "You will stay here," she said simply.

"What? Where's my father?" said Sport.

"You are to stay here," she repeated. "The hotel is instructed to accept no outgoing calls, so you needn't try calling." She gathered her fur around her and went toward the door. She was leaving! She was leaving him in that room! Sport ran toward her.

"What are you doing?" he yelled.

She turned around quickly as though she thought he might hit her. Her eyes flashed. "It will all be settled in about a week. Until then, you're to stay

here. You'll miss school, but you won't mind that."
She smiled a nasty little smile. "You can have anything you want on room service"—she paused—
"but don't try to get away. It's all been taken care
of. You can't."

She opened the door, locked it behind her, and
was gone.

Sport stood looking at the closed door. He felt
numb. He felt that the whole thing wasn't happening to him. He sat down on the bed and looked
around the room. It was all gold. The rug,
draperies, and bedspread were a dull gold, the
headboards some kind of rubbed wood. There was
a great oval antique mirror across from him in
which he suddenly saw himself, his eyes wide, his
face pale and smaller than he had ever seen it.

His father had once said to him, and he remembered it now, "If you are ever in real trouble, don't
panic. Sit down and think about it. Remember
two things, always. There must be some way out
of it and there must be humor in it somewhere."

Ech, thought Sport. There wasn't anything
funny about this and there wasn't any way out
of it.

After all, though, he told himself calmly, it
wasn't really a prison. It was a hotel in the biggest
city in the world.

He ran to the window. It took a lot of strength
to raise it, but he did at last. He tried to lean out.

There was a piece of slanting glass stopping him. He leaned further.

"*Help!*" he screamed. "*Help! Help!*" He felt foolish at first but when he got going, he didn't anymore, and screamed for all he was worth. "*Help! Help! Help!*"

Through his screams he saw the little ant people, the toy cars, the tiny awnings, the baby trees that looked as though they belonged along a toy railroad. It took a few minutes to penetrate, but the scream died in his throat as he realized that he was too high up for anyone ever to hear him. For one mad moment he considered climbing out onto the ledge, but even the thought made him dizzy. If they didn't hear him, then chances were they wouldn't see him either, and he'd just have to crawl back in. He turned away from the window.

He went to the telephone.

"May I help you?" said a woman's voice.

"I want to call RE seven, four-eight-three-three," he said, giving his father's number and trying to sound old.

There was a pause. Sport held his breath. Maybe she lied, he thought quickly.

Then: "I can connect you with room service, young fellow, but that's all." The voice sounded rather sympathetic.

"Thank you," said Sport, and hung up.

He looked around the room. He tried the door even though he knew it was useless.

He sat down again. Suddenly he jumped up. He ran into the bathroom and looked around. He ran to his suitcase and opened it up. He rummaged through it, finally took out one of his sneakers. There was a pad and pencil next to the telephone. He wrote on the pad hurriedly, "I AM TRAPPED IN . . ." He didn't know the room number. He ran to the back of the door and looked at the framed card. He ran back and wrote:

I AM TRAPPED IN ROOM 1607.
PLEASE CALL MY FATHER AT RE 7-4833
AND TELL HIM TO COME GET ME.

He put the note in the sneaker with just enough sticking out so someone would see it.

He ran to the window, leaned over the glass thing as far as he could, and aimed right at the doorman's head. The sneaker flew through the air in a dizzying spiral, getting smaller and smaller until it landed with a small indentation on the top of the awning and sat forlornly holding its message.

Sport felt horribly empty as he leaned back into the room.

"All I did was throw my sneaker out the window," he said aloud, and suddenly it seemed funny. What do you do with one sneaker? he asked himself, and laughed at that. "I'm only a bird in a gilded cage," he sang loudly, and laughed again. Maybe, he thought slowly, maybe if I make a lot of noise inside the room, someone will notice.

Having decided upon this, he started to scream as loud as he could. He picked up his suitcase and threw it against the outside door. He pushed a chair over. He stomped on the floor, jumping up and down and using his whole weight on both feet.

He stopped, exhausted, having nothing else to throw. Silence greeted him. It was the same silence that had been there before he started to yell.

He sat down. Maybe he was the only one on this floor. Maybe nobody ever come up here. Waiters had to deliver things, though. He jumped up, ran over, picked up the phone, and shouted, "Room service."

A voice said, "Room service. May I help you?"

"Yes," said Sport, beginning to smile. "I'd like the biggest steak you've got."

"Certainly. What would you like with that?"

"Potatoes and a malted," said Sport.

"I beg your pardon?"

"A malted, a black and white malted," said Sport.

"Yes, sir, and what dressing on your salad?"

"What?"

"French, Roquefort, or house?"

"House?" He saw a house sitting on a salad.

"Yes, sir, and how would you like your steak?"

"Right now."

"Rare, medium, or well done?"

"Oh, medium."

"Your room number, please?"

"Sixteen-oh-seven. And some rolls, too."

"Rolls come with it, sir. Would you like some special kind of rolls? We have hard rolls or . . ."

"Any kind," said Sport, "and can you hurry?"

"We will fill your order as soon as possible, sir. We're doing the breakfast orders now. Nine o'clock in the morning, I don't mind telling you, we don't get many calls for steak. It will be along as soon as possible."

"Thank you," said Sport.

He hung up the phone. He was suddenly starving.

As he waited for the food, he made his plans. Forty-five minutes later when it came, he was ready.

The buzzer sounded. Sport stood up and ran over to the closet door which was between the bathroom and the outside door. He stepped inside, leaving the door open a crack. He heard a key unlock the front door. He saw a waiter pushing in a long table covered with a white cloth. On top were silver dishes with lids on them.

Just as the waiter got through the door, Sport

pushed open the closet door and dove through the open front door.

He was in the hall. A hand grabbed the back of his collar. "And where are we going?" growled a voice above the hand.

Sport twisted like a fish. The hand let go, then two hands grasped his shoulders and turned him around.

He looked up into the face of a man who wore a hat down over one eye and had a cigarette hanging out of his mouth.

"Think you'll just split, huh?" said the man.

"Who are you?" said Sport.

"I'm here to see you don't leave," said the man.

Sport then noticed a chair that was placed right outside the door.

The man pushed Sport ahead of him back into the room. He held on to Sport. The waiter was still there.

"Sign the tab," said the man.

The waiter held out a piece of paper to Sport.

"What?" said Sport.

"Just sign your name," said the man with the hat. "They'll tip you later," he said to the waiter. The waiter nodded.

Sport took the pencil and wrote "Simon Rocque" on the card.

He noticed that the bill was fifteen dollars, two dollars for the malted. "Geez," he said loudly.

The waiter bowed out of the room. The man in the hat let Sport go. "Don't try it again, sonny," he said as he went toward the door. "I'm right out there, day and night. No use making all that noise either. Nobody going to do anything no matter how much you make." He went out the door, leaving behind the smell of smoke. The lock turned once again.

Sport went over to the table and sat down. He ate everything. The steak was great and so was the malted. After he ate he went over and lay down on the bed. He fell asleep almost immediately.

Chapter 19

At the end of three days Sport was so sick of
steak that he never wanted to see one again. He
had had steak three times a day for three days. He
decided, on the morning of the fourth day, that he
would systematically have everything printed on
the menu. That day at lunch he ordered demitasse
for dessert and discovered it was coffee. After that
he stuck to the things that sounded familiar.

The detective outside the door had brought him
some magazines to read. There was a television in
the room and he watched that, all day and late into
the night, falling asleep in the middle of *The Late
Show*. He decided that the detective must come
in and turn it off because it was always off in the
morning.

On the afternoon of the fourth day a package
arrived from Brooks Brothers with new shirts and
new underwear. Sport just looked at it. He kept on
the same clothes he had arrived in. He had the

feeling that if he stayed dressed, he might leave any minute.

That evening, after he had had dinner, he sat watching television. He heard the door unlock. Figuring that it was the busboy to take away the dinner table, he didn't stop looking at the television until he heard voices outside the door.

"I'm gonna step down the lobby," he heard the detective say. "He ain't to leave here. You wait'll I come back."

"Yes, sir. Thank you, sir," said a strangely familiar voice.

Sport heard the heavy feet of the detective clump down the hall. The door edged open and Chi-chi walked into the room.

"Chi—" Sport only got half the name out because Chi-chi put his finger to his lips. He wore a busboy's uniform.

He closed the door behind him. "Geez," he whispered, "I knew they had a kid up here. I didn't know it was you all this time."

"I gotta get out," whispered Sport.

"Who put you here?" said Chi-chi.

"My blanking mother. I gotta get back. My father doesn't know where I am, I bet."

Chi-chi looked thoughtful. He took off his jacket. "Try this," he said quickly.

Sport tried it, but couldn't get into it because it was too small.

"I know," said Chi-chi. "I saw it in a movie once." He lifted up the long white cloth on the table. He took out the big steel warmer where the hot food was kept. There was a small shelf where the warmer had sat.

"There!" said Chi-chi.

"Yeah!" said Sport.

Chi-chi put the warmer in the bathroom and closed the door.

"You crawl in," said Chi-chi, "then I lower the sides and the cloth'll cover you." Chi-chi pointed to the shelf.

Sport crawled under and made himself as small as possible. Chi-chi moved the plates around on top of the table so he could lower the two sides. The sides were lowered, making even less room for Sport.

"Hurry," he whispered to Chi-chi.

"All set," said Chi-chi and started toward the door. "Hang on," he whispered.

Sport heard him open the outside door. As they bumped over the sill, Sport's heart leaped in fear at the sound of the detective's voice.

"Where is he?" he said.

"In the john," said Chi-chi calmly.

"Oh, okay," said the detective.

Sport held his breath as he continued to roll down the hall away from the door. He could hear the detective lock the door again, the chair hit the wall as he sat down again.

He felt himself turn a corner. The table stopped.

"It's the elevator," whispered Chi-chi. "Keep quiet."

Sport heard the elevator open, and felt the table roll forward. The elevator went down. The doors opened again and the table rolled out. It rolled for a long time then, past lot of banging of pots and pans and the chatter of voices. It rolled at last into a room that was quiet, and Sport heard a door shut.

Chi-chi lifted the cloth. "Quick, now," he said. "We gotta get you out before he gets wise."

The fresh air felt great to Sport after the closed-in table. He took a deep breath and looked around. They were in a small room with a lot of lockers. "Where are we?" he asked Chi-chi, who was rummaging through a pile of clothes.

"Here. This oughta fit," he said. "Put it on." He held out a busboy's uniform. Sport started to take his clothes off.

"Quick," said Chi-chi. "I'm not supposed to have the table in here."

Sport got the uniform on. Chi-chi wadded up the old clothes and put them in a locker.

"Come on, now. Just follow me and don't say anything to anybody."

Chi-chi wheeled the table out the door and along a small passageway to another room which was filled with similar dirty tables. He shoved the table over next to them.

"Now come on," he said to Sport.

Sport followed him out, down the hall, past a whole line of garbage pails, up a ramp to a door that led to the street. There was a man at this door, sitting at a table.

"He's just going across the street," said Chi-chi.

"What for?" said the man.

"Mr. Hargrove sent him," said Chi-chi. "He's supposed to pick up something."

"Okay," said the man, looking at Sport.

Sport didn't look at him.

"He's new?" said the man.

"Yeah," said Chi-chi. "Started yesterday."

"Okay," said the man. Lumbering to his feet, the man opened the big outside door.

"See ya, Sport," said Chi-chi as the big door rumbled open and Sport stepped out into the air.

"Yeah, Chi-chi," said Sport. He was afraid to look back because of the man. He looked straight ahead into Fifty-eighth Street, which had never looked so beautiful.

He went toward Sixth Avenue because he didn't want to pass the front of the hotel.

When he figured the man couldn't see him anymore, he ran as fast as he could. It was around eight o'clock at night and there were still a lot of people on the streets. He dodged in and out of the people on the sidewalk, running as fast as he could.

He got to the corner and hailed a cab. I don't have a cent, he thought as he got into the cab. He told the cab driver his address, and, sitting back, he began to breathe again. He decided that he would ask the cab driver to wait while he ran up and got the money from his father. The fact that his father and Kate might not be home ran through his mind, but he couldn't let it stay there because it was too frightening.

The cab plunged into the park. It was dark and the weather had begun to be cold. Sport shivered. If they're not home . . . he began in his mind, then pushed it down again. The cab was on the East Side now heading toward the river. Sport found he was holding his breath again. He let it out and took a deep breath. Soon, he thought, soon.

The cab pulled up in front of his house. There was a light on in his apartment!

"I'll be right back down," said Sport hurriedly, getting out of the cab.

"Hey, what is this?" yelled the cab driver, but he was too late. Sport was already up the steps and in the front door. He ran as fast as he could up the steps and pounded on the door, almost throwing his body against it.

"What's that?" he heard Kate say.

"ME! ME!" yelled Sport as loud as he could.

The door was flung open and his father grabbed him up in his arms.

"Sport!" cried Kate.

His father held him so hard against his shoulder that Sport thought he would suffocate. He didn't care, though. He felt his eyes fill with tears. He saw Kate over his father's shoulder, and she was crying.

"Ruumph," said his father, putting him down and blowing his nose in a large handkerchief.

Kate grabbed him then, hugged him hard. He hugged her back, smelling her perfume and trying not to cry.

"Where'd they have you?" said his father, turning around. Sport saw that his eyes were red.

"The Plaza," said Sport.

His father blew his nose again and burst out laughing. "The *Plaza!*" he cried, laughing.

"We've been out of our minds," said Kate.

"HEY!" came a loud shout from downstairs.

"Oh, geez, Dad, the taxi man. I didn't have any money," said Sport.

"Oh," said his father. He went to the door. "Hold it," he yelled as he ran down the steps.

"Are you okay?" said Kate, looking him over, her face serious, concerned.

"Sure," said Sport.

"You look like you just came out of the dryer at the Laundromat," said Kate, touching the collar of his shirt tenderly.

"What? Oh," said Sport, looking down at the messy uniform.

Sport started to laugh and couldn't stop. He was still laughing when his father came back in the room. His father went to Kate and gave her a hug.

"What a relief," said Kate.

"Yeah," said Mr. Rocque, looking angry. "I'll fix that dame if it's the last thing I do."

"You hungry, Sport?" asked Kate.

"No," said Sport, weak from laughing. "I had steak every day," he said and started laughing again even though it wasn't funny. He laughed and laughed.

"Easy now," said Mr. Rocque.

"He's tired," said Kate.

"Come on, son," said Mr. Rocque and grabbed Sport up in his arms as though he were a little baby. "Easy does it. Snap out of it."

Sport stopped laughing. His father hugged him once and put him down.

"I think maybe a glass of hot milk," said Kate, going into the kitchen.

"Make it a round of hot milk," said Mr. Rocque,

running his hand through Sport's hair. "You could use a bath," he said gently.

"Or hot chocolate. Like that?" asked Kate from the kitchen.

"Yeah!" said Sport and Mr. Rocque at the same time. They looked at each other and laughed.

Chapter 20

Sport fell asleep without even finishing his hot chocolate. His father picked him up and put him into bed.

In the morning he awoke to the smell of bacon frying. He lay in bed looking around the room. Everything seemed good. The good feel of the bed, the bacon smells, his old desk. He bounded out of bed and into the kitchen.

"Good morning!" said Kate happily. "Room service may have more variety but . . ."

"Oh, boy, bacon," said Sport and sat down.

". . . at least we're clean," finished Kate, looking pointedly at Sport.

Sport was eating bacon happily.

"I say, old bean, did you bathe any one of those five days you were sitting in the lap of luxury?" Kate squinted her eyes and tried to look mean.

"Oh, rats," said Sport.

"Rats is what you're going to have in your ears if you don't bathe right after breakfast."

"Huumph," said Sport, with his mouth full and feeling thoroughly happy. "Where's Dad?"

"Your dad is down at his lawyer's office signing some very important papers that say little boys cannot be kept in the Plaza." Kate sat down with her cup of coffee.

"What happened?" said Sport. "Why did she do that?"

"She put you in one room and herself in another room and told everybody she had taken you to Paris."

"Yeah? What for?" Sport stopped eating.

"Wilton tried to find you and naturally when we got back, we were frantic and wanted to call the police."

Sport had a vision of the cops entering the hotel room with drawn guns scaring the detective to death.

"Then it turns out Charlotte had hired another lawyer and is suing for your custody, your complete custody, not any of this half-a-year business."

"What for? She hates me."

"Greedy. She's greedy. She figured that with your custody she'd get all the money. She had big plans for saying your father was a bum, that I'm worse, that we give wild parties with artists all over the place doing dirty things."

Sport laughed.

"She had big plans, that lady." Kate took a swallow of coffee. "Only now she's going to end up with, we hope, nothing."

"What are we gonna do?" asked Sport.

"Your father is countersuing for your custody and he'll get it. You can't just kidnap a person even if he's your own son. She was supposed to return you to your father after that week was out."

"You mean she was gonna take me just to get the money?"

"It's a lot of money, baby, and when there's a lot of money involved, some people turn into pigs."

"Is she not gonna get any of it now?"

"I imagine she'll get the fourth, but she won't get half, and she won't get the whole shebang, which is what she wanted."

"What does Mr. Wilton say?" He remembered hearing his father call Wilton the night before and say, "He's home."

"Wilton was appalled. He wouldn't have had anything to do with her carryings-on, of course. That's why she had to get another lawyer. The other lawyer's a sneaky little rat who'd do anything for that much money. When he started calling up

Wilton and your father's lawyer, we knew you were safe somewhere, but we didn't know where or how we'd ever find you until the whole thing came to court. She could have stayed in the Plaza under another name from now till Doomsday if she never went out, and never let you get out. Thank God for Chi-chi."

"I'm gonna have a lot of homework to do," said Sport.

"You're gonna have a lot of bathing to do, and I mean right now."

"Drat."

"Drat yourself right into that shower," said Kate, getting up and taking the dishes to the sink.

Sport moved slowly toward the bathroom. He didn't mind bathing. He didn't mind anything if he could just stay there forever. He ran his finger along the dull ocher of the walls, around the corner, past his father's room, and down the hall to the blue-tiled bathroom. He remembered the man who put the tile in, because before that there had been just plaster walls. He remembered how happy he and his father had been to have a tiled bathroom. He thought of the bathroom at the Plaza and how he hated it. Turning on the shower, he thought of the wildly fancy bathroom at Charlotte's house. It was funny to think of, but the bathrooms he liked weren't fancy; this one, and the one at Seymour's, and the one at Harry's. They weren't fancy, but they were home. He got in the shower. The one squirt that always went haywire hit him right in the eye. He laughed up into the warm water running over his ears.

"I got rats in my ears," he sang loudly, imitating his father in the shower, ". . . rats . . . in . . . my . . . ears."

Chapter 21

That afternoon Sport walked down York Avenue toward his school. He felt good after his shower. He had on clean jeans that Kate had taken to the Laundromat for him while he was away. He passed the stationery store and waved at the counter man. He passed O'Neil's candy store and waved at Mrs. O'Neil through the window. Mrs. O'Neil looked startled and ran out onto the sidewalk wiping her hands on her white apron.

"Where you been? Everybody's looking high and low for you!" She grabbed him by the shirt collar as though he were going to run away. "Your father know where you are?"

Sport laughed. "Yeah. They found me. It's okay."

She let him go and smiled down at him. "Where were you? You run away?"

"No. My mother had me locked up in the Plaza."

"The Plaza Hotel? Ooh-la-la."

"Yeah. Chi-chi got me out."

"Chi-chi Ramon? That little squirt? How'd he do that?"

"Put me under the room service wagon. He's a busboy."

"Glory be to God," said Mrs. O'Neil. "And it's a wonder your poor father didn't lose his hair. He came by, you know, looking for you. Where you going now? Want a sweet roll?"

"Sure," said Sport and followed her in. She handed him a sweet roll from one of the glass containers. "I'm going to school to see the fellas," said Sport, eating happily.

"Seymour'll be glad to see you," said Mrs. O'Neil, looking vague because a customer had just come in. "You're a good friend," she said over her shoulder, going toward the man at the counter.

"See ya," said Sport and bounded out the door. He walked along the street finishing the roll.

As he got near the school he could see everybody start to come out the door. School was out for lunch and everyone bounced out, swinging bookbags, chasing each other, and giving loud whoops. Sport started to run.

"Hey, Seymour," he yelled as he ran across Seventy-ninth Street.

"Hey, Sport," yelled Seymour and Harry, who were coming out the door. Chi-chi was behind them.

"Hey, did Chi-chi tell ya?" yelled Sport, running up to them.

"Yeah," said Seymour.

"Crazy," said Harry.

"Hi," said Chi-chi, looking like a hero.

"Long as you were there," said Seymour, "I told Chi-chi, whyncha steal the silver at least."

"Lose my job, what else?" said Chi-chi.

"Meet any of those crazy ladies in the halls?" asked Harry.

"I couldn't even get to the halls," said Sport. "Where you guys going?"

"The park," said Seymour.

"I'm starving," said Harry.

"I'm not, your ma just gave me a roll," said Sport to Seymour.

"Come on, let's go there, she'll feed us," said Seymour.

"Yeah, man," said Harry.

"I got no money," said Chi-chi.

"You don't need none," said Seymour.

They started off, playing ball as they went. Sport could throw the longest so he got farther away. He was a long way up the block with Seymour at the other end and Harry and Chi-chi in the middle. Harry was so tall he jumped up and caught the high throws, and Chi-chi couldn't throw very well so he got the ground balls. They walked this way up the sidewalk, laughing and yelling, irritating several old ladies and causing a lady with a baby carriage, who had had to duck, to scream at them.

"Off the sidewalk!" she yelled. "You got no right!" Seymour started to yell at her and Harry and Chi-chi were watching.

A long black car pulled up to the sidewalk right next to Sport. He didn't even see what happened. Before he knew it, the door had opened, a long arm had grabbed him in, and he was sitting in the backseat next to Carrie with the car moving rapidly away from the curb.

"Harry!" Sport shouted as loud as he could. He thought Harry turned around, but he wasn't sure.

"Sit down and shut up," said Carrie. She grabbed him with a long, freckled hand.

"Get away from me," yelled Sport in a frenzy.

The car stopped for a red light. Sport lunged for the door and got it open. Carrie was holding onto the end of his coat. He started to scream as loud as he could. "Help! Help!"

Egbert put the brake on, got out, and ran around the car. He started to push Sport back in the car and close the door. Out of the corner of his eye Sport could see Harry running as fast as he could toward the car. Seymour and Chi-chi were behind him.

"Help! Murder!" yelled Sport. He pushed with all his might against Carrie and managed to kick Egbert in the stomach.

"Let go that kid," yelled Harry, pounding up to the car and pulling the door back away from Egbert.

Seymour came up and grabbed Egbert's coat.

"Madam!" shrieked Egbert in a high voice. It was the first word Sport had ever heard him say and it sounded rather pitiful. Harry grabbed Egbert by the hair and pulled him back. Sport kept kicking as hard as he could. Seymour was pulling the door out of Egbert's hand and Chi-chi was trying to pull Sport away from Carrie.

There was a siren whine. Sport felt himself released by Carrie, so suddenly that Chi-chi had pulled him out onto the sidewalk before he knew what had happened. Two policemen jumped out of a squad car leaving the doors open. Egbert gave Harry a swat, but Harry ducked.

Sport looked up out of the gutter and saw a cop standing over him. "Break it up! Break it up!" Both cops were yelling and pulling everybody around.

"Hey, wait a minute!" yelled Harry as a cop pulled him away from the car and held him in one hand while he grabbed Seymour with the other. The other cop picked up Sport and Chi-chi, holding them both by their shirts.

"Hey, you're ripping my shirt," yelled Seymour.

Egbert was brushing off his uniform.

"What happened here?" said the first cop.

Egbert looked into the interior of the car.

"We were attacked," said Carrie in a quavering voice. "We were brutally attacked by this gang as we stopped for the red light."

"That's a lie!" yelled Sport.

"Keep your mouth shut, sonny," said the cop loudly.

"They tried to get him in the car," yelled Seymour.

"I said shut up!" yelled the cop. "Let the lady talk."

"They swarmed around us . . ." said Carrie in a helpless voice. ". . . My chauffeur was trying to fight them off."

"Why, you blanking . . ." yelled Seymour. "I'll punch you right in the nose."

"You'll punch nobody," boomed the cop. "Come along." He started to shove Seymour and Sport toward the patrol car.

Harry and Chi-chi weren't saying anything. They were shoved ahead, still silent, into the waiting car. The cop got in the front seat and turned around and glared at them. "What's a matter with you rotten trash?" he growled, his mouth half closed.

"She's lying!" yelled Sport.

"Keep quiet," said Harry under his breath.

"That's right," said the cop, "listen to your buddy there. He's been in trouble before, he knows."

"I have not," said Harry.

"Watch yourself, nigger baby," said the cop.

The other cop, who had been talking to Carrie, came back to the squad car and got in. The long black limousine rolled away, free.

"All right, let's take 'em in," said the first cop.

The squad car started off. They went slowly. The second cop turned around and faced the boys. He seemed to have a better face than the other one.

"We're taking you in because you cannot hold up cars at red lights," he said sweetly.

"That's not what happened," said Sport.

"Shut up," said the first cop, who was driving.

"What are you saying, sonny?" said the second cop.

"That's his aunt!" yelled Seymour, beside himself.

"Cool it," said Chi-chi.

"You," said the second cop, pointing to Sport, "what are you saying?"

"That was my aunt," said Sport, "she was trying . . ."

"Your aunt, my foot," said the first cop. "That lady never saw scum like you."

The second cop pointed silently to Sport again.

"She was trying to kidnap me," said Sport.

"Oh?" said the second cop delicately, arching his eyebrows.

"I've heard 'em all," said the first cop.

"It's true!" yelled Seymour.

"And who might you be that anyone might want to kidnap you?" asked the second cop, mincing his speech.

Sport thought quickly. "My name is Simon Rocque. I'm Chester Vane's grandson."

"Oh, boy, that takes the cake," said the first cop.

"He is!" yelled Seymour.

The second cop turned his back on the boys and said in an undertone to the first cop, "That was Vane's car and chauffeur."

"What's that?" muttered the first cop.

"My mother's trying to get my custody," said Sport loudly. "She already kidnapped me once, and that was my aunt doing the same thing."

"He's dead as a mackerel, Chester Vane," muttered the first cop.

"We better not risk it," said the second cop. He turned back to Sport. "How's your grandfather doing? I heard he was sick."

"He's dead," said Sport.

"What's your mother's name?"

"Charlotte Vane, and that's her sister Carrie."

"Where do you live?"

"Eighty-second Street between York and East End."

"The Vanes don't live there."

"I know it," said Sport. "I live with my father."

"What's your father's name?"

"Matthew Rocque."

"Your mother at home now?"

"How do I know?" said Sport.

"Drive by the Vanes'," said the second cop.

The squad car turned downtown. Harry nudged Sport and winked at him. Seymour looked very mad. Chi-chi looked bland, as though he were taking a carriage ride through Central Park.

The car pulled up in front of the Vane house. The long limousine was sitting in front, empty.

The second cop unlocked the back door, pulled Sport out, slammed the door, and locked it again. The first cop cut the motor and turned in his seat to snarl at the three boys. "I suppose you're all Rockefellers."

The second cop pushed Sport gently up the steps. He rang the bell.

After a few minutes, Howard opened the door.

"Why, Mister Simon, hello," he said, looking at Sport.

"Is this boy related to the Vanes?" asked the second cop.

"Why, yes, sir," said Howard, looking at the cop in a shocked way. "He's Miss Charlotte's boy."

"Is Miss Charlotte Vane at home?"

"Yes, sir," said Howard, opening the door and letting Sport and the cop into the dim cool hallway.

"I will tell her you're here," said Howard, and bowed toward the door to the library. He went inside and closed it behind him.

The cop relaxed his hold on Sport. Sport put his shirt back in place.

After a minute Charlotte opened the door and swept out.

"Officer," she said grandly, holding out her hand as though the cop would kiss it. "I'm so glad to see you. There's been this terrible incident. I'm so glad that Simon is safe. You see, my sister has not been well. There are days when . . . well, when she doesn't even recognize me." Charlotte looked terribly sad.

"This boy says he's your son," said the cop doggedly.

"Why, of course he is," said Charlotte airily. "And I'm terribly sorry to have put you to this trouble."

"He says that he was being kidnapped," said the cop.

"Why, how perfectly ridiculous," said Charlotte.

"He wasn't being kidnapped?" said the cop.

"Of course not," said Charlotte. "Run along inside, Simon, have cook give you a sandwich."

Sport didn't budge. "She's lying!" he yelled suddenly.

"Si-mon," whined Charlotte in a haunting way, "you know how we feel about these little white lies . . ."

"Oh-ho," said the cop.

"I want to see my father," said Sport.

"Your father is coming over shortly to discuss some things, dear," said Charlotte. "You can see him then." She managed somehow to twine her arm around Sport and pull him gently to her side.

"I want to go home," said Sport loudly.

"There's no one there, darling, you know that," cooed Charlotte, the very picture of a loving mother.

"There is so!" yelled Sport, pulling away from Charlotte and standing near the cop.

"Have you got your bus card on you?" asked the cop.

"Sure," said Sport and pulled out the card that let him, as a schoolchild, get on buses free.

The cop looked it over and handed it back.

"I think, Miss Vane, that I had better return the boy to his house." He started to put his cap back on, then stopped, waving it around uncertainly.

"This is equally his house," Charlotte said harshly.

"I am supposed to return a lost child to the address which is listed as his home address . . ."

"I am his mother," said Charlotte, shrill now.

". . . and to no other address," the cop said and turned toward the door, propelling Sport before him.

"This is absurd," said Charlotte strongly. "Who is your superior officer? I will report you."

"Captain Jensen, ma'am, Nineteenth Precinct," said the cop in a bored way as he opened the front door.

"I will call him immediately," said Charlotte, slamming the door.

"Call away," muttered the cop as he led Sport back to the squad car.

He put Sport in the back and got into the front seat.

"Something fishy," he said to the first cop.

"See, I told ya . . ." said the first cop.

"No. He is her son, but something doesn't smell right."

"It's the backseat."

"Cut it out, Charlie. Let's take the kid home and talk to the father."

"What'll we do with the rest of Ellis Island back there?"

"We'll figure it out when we get there. No one has pressed any charges anyway."

Sport felt Harry's body relax.

"Whyncha let us out?" said Seymour loudly. "We ain't done nothing."

The cop started the car. "Shut your mouth," he said shortly.

It was hot in the backseat. Nobody spoke until they got near Eighty-second Street.

"Where does he live?" asked the first cop. The second cop told him.

"Figures," said the first cop.

"Listen you . . ." said Seymour. Harry gave him a sharp dig in the ribs.

"I'm listening," said the first cop.

"Let's everybody take it easy," said the second cop. "Here's the house."

The second cop got out, unlocked the back door again, and Sport got out.

"What's gonna happen to them?" he asked, pointing to his friends.

"Take it easy," said the second cop. "We'll get this straightened out."

He took Sport up the steps to his apartment.

Chapter 22

In front of the door they passed Mr. Collins. "Hah!" he said loudly. "I knew it would happen. Happens every time. Cop gets 'em every time."

The policeman ignored him and knocked on the door of the apartment.

Sport held his breath, hoping his father was home. The door swung open finally, revealing Mr. Rocque with his mouth full, chewing madly. "Aaagh," he said when he saw the cop. He saw Sport then, swallowed everything in a gulp and said, "What's this?" too loudly.

"Dad!" said Sport rather wildly.

"Wait a minute," said the cop. "This your son?" he asked Mr. Rocque.

"Of course. What happened?"

"Well . . ." began the cop.

"Oh, come in," said Mr. Rocque.

The cop pushed Sport ahead of him through

the door. Mr. Rocque closed the door. Sport could see Kate at the kitchen door, her eyes wide.

"You been having some trouble with your wife?" asked the cop, glancing toward Kate. He took off his cap and rocked back and forth on his heels.

"What is this? What are you talking about?" said Mr. Rocque, exasperated.

"Carrie tried to kidnap me!" yelled Sport.

"What?" said Mr. Rocque loudly.

"Again?" said Kate from the doorway. She came into the room.

"What the hell happened?" said Mr. Rocque, getting very agitated. "I'm calling my lawyer right now." He was at the phone in two steps. "This has gone far enough. This'll do it. She's had it." He was dialing rapidly. Kate came and put her arm around Sport.

"What happened, Officer?" she said coolly.

"Well. There was a commotion on the street and we come along and find this boy and three others in a fight with a chauffeur. The lady in the car says they were attacked. This boys says they tried to kidnap him."

"They got Seymour and Harry and Chi-chi in the squad car!" said Sport frantically.

"Downstairs?" asked Kate, looking at Sport.

"Yeah! Can't they get out, Kate?"

"I just want to clear up . . ." began the cop.

"Have those boys been charged with anything?" asked Kate.

"No," said the cop.

"Sam," screamed Mr. Rocque into the phone. "She's done it again. She's tried to take my boy, and I've had it."

"Then I think they should be released," said Kate calmly.

"Well . . ." said the cop.

"The officer is right here in the room. She's got to be stopped, Sam. I can't have my boy scared to go out in the street," yelled Mr. Rocque. "She's ruthless. She'll do any damn thing."

"Can't you let them go? They didn't do nothing," pleaded Sport. "They were trying to help me is all."

The officer ignored him, looked over his head at Mr. Rocque, listening. Mr. Rocque was silent, the phone pushed into his ear, his other arm making gestures as though he were pleading a case in court.

"Sam. That's all well and good," he said finally, trying to be patient, "but I want something *now*, this minute, an injunction or something, something that'll stop her."

There was another silence and everyone waited, looking at Mr. Rocque.

"Oh . . . yeah, the papers," he said slowly. He

nodded his head over and over again until he looked like a doll on a stick. "That's all I want, just an assurance, just that she hasn't got a chance," he said finally. "Okay, Sam, yeah, I'll talk to the officer. Yeah, I'll call you back. Good-bye."

He faced them but seemed to see only the officer. "Now," he said in a determined voice. "I'd like to know exactly what happened."

The officer related what he had seen and what he had done so far.

"The kids are still in the squad car, Dad!" said Sport.

"Let's get them out of there," said Mr. Rocque to the cop. "They haven't done anything."

"They tried to help me is all," said Sport.

"There aren't any charges . . ." began the cop reluctantly.

"Then let's get them out," said Mr. Rocque.

". . . but I think a few strong words about attacking . . ." The cop seemed confused.

"Look," said Mr. Rocque patiently, "they didn't attack anyone. They were attacked."

"Still . . ." The cop was looking at the floor. "There was a pretty big brawl going on there when we got there."

"I am perfectly capable of teaching my son not to get in fights, Officer," said Mr. Rocque stiffly. "If there are any strong words, I'll say them. These boys you mention are good boys. They don't get into trouble. Not one of them has ever been in trouble, right, Sport?"

"No," said Sport loudly. "And they didn't do anything this time either."

"I'll let them go when I get down to the car," said the officer, taking a little black leather note-book and a pencil out of his back pocket. "I want to get my report straight." He started all over again with Mr. Rocque who started all over again, patiently explaining.

Kate took Sport into the kitchen. "Sit down," she whispered, "and be patient. They're all slow. The guys'll get out. Just wait a minute. You hungry?"

Sport sat down. "No," he said sadly.

"That's news," said Kate. "Did they hurt you?"

"That ol' lady twisted my arm," said Sport.

"Really? Does it hurt? Why didn't you say so?"

"I didn't have time to say anything," said Sport loudly.

"Let me see," said Kate, lifting Sport's arm up and down and asking, "Does it hurt this way?"

Sport said yes to almost every position she put it in. It did hurt badly.

Kate went into the living room. "I think you should know . . ." she said to Mr. Rocque and the officer. "The boy's arm is hurt. He says Carrie did it."

"What? What?" yelled Mr. Rocque.

"Easy, Matthew," said Kate. "It's probably just

a sprain. I think he should be checked, but what I means is, I think this should be in the report."

The cop wrote it down.

"I can't believe them," said Mr. Rocque. His face was white with rage.

"You want to press charges?" asked the cop.

"Yes, I want to press charges," said Mr. Rocque loudly. "Kidnapping and assault and battery and anything you can think of . . ." Mr. Rocque was shaking and stuttering with rage.

"Do you think you should call your lawyer back?" said Kate.

"Listen . . ." said Mr. Rocque. "They're gonna come smelling around . . ." He pointed his finger at the cop. "They're gonna come around trying to keep this out of the papers . . ."

"Not a chance," said the cop, and laughed. Sport poked his head out of the kitchen. Suddenly he was so angry he couldn't contain himself. He stood up and yelled as loud as he could. "Get those guys outa that squad car. They haven't done NOTHING."

He looked in wonder at the adults who stared at him. He started to shake. He continued to stand there shaking.

"I'll go downstairs with you," said Mr. Rocque. He opened the door.

"Your name is Miss . . ." said the cop to Kate.

"Mrs. Rocque," said Mr. Rocque in a very loud, angry voice.

"Mrs. Rocque," said the cop and wrote it down. "I think that's all," he said calmly and put the little book back in his pocket.

He tipped his hat to Kate. "Mrs. Rocque," he said and turned toward the door. "Stay outa trouble, sonny," he said to Sport and followed Mr. Rocque downstairs. The door shut behind them.

"Ech!" said Sport.

"You know what happened to the snakes when Saint Patrick drove them out of Ireland?" said Kate, laughing and coming into the kitchen.

"What?" said Sport.

"They all swam over and became the New York Police Force."

Sport started laughing very hard and then he was crying with nothing in between. Kate held his head. He tried to stuff down the tears, but he couldn't. He heard steps outside the door. He pulled his head away and wiped his face on his sleeve.

"Don't worry," said Kate. "Every man cries once in a while."

The front door banged open and Seymour jumped in, followed by Harry, Chi-chi, and Mr. Rocque.

"Hey, Sport," yelled Seymour. "You shoulda seen

your dad with the fuzz!" Seymour looked admiringly at Mr. Rocque.

"Yeah!" said Harry. "Didn't give an inch."

"You oughta seen it," said Chi-chi. "They wanted our names and addresses . . ."

". . . and families," said Harry.

". . . and he wouldn't let 'em take anything!" said Seymour happily.

"Why?" asked Kate.

"Oh, you know," said Mr. Rocque, "they say they just want names to have in their reports but what they do is, when something happens in this neighborhood they come looking for these kids and say they've been in trouble before."

"Why?" said Sport.

"Because they're lazy," said Mr. Rocque. "This way they don't have to think."

"Geez, you know what he did?" said Seymour.

"Yeah," said Harry. Even Harry was impressed, and Sport had never seen Harry impressed by anything.

"What?" said Sport.

"He told them they oughta be glad nobody presses charges on them for picking us up, said they didn't even try to understand the situation, but just sided with a rich lady in a limousine because she was a rich lady in a limousine, said what kind of values they expect us to have when cops do things like that." Seymour looked terribly proud.

"What did they say?" asked Sport, looking at Mr. Rocque. Mr. Rocque looked away with a little smile. Kate winked at him.

"They huffed and they puffed," said Harry.

"That rotten one, you know, the one driving," said Seymour, "he started to say something rotten to your dad and the other guy waved his hand at him and shut him up. Then the other one, the one that come up here, says, 'Come on everybody, outa the car,' just like that, and we got out. Your dad told us to come up here." Seymour looked like he had won a raffle.

"They don't like Puerto Ricans much," said Chi-chi quietly with a little smile.

"Aw, they're mad for Blacks," said Harry, poking Chi-chi.

"They have a hard time, too," said Kate. "There's so much crime in this city, they get like the criminals."

"Oh, poof," said Mr. Rocque.

Kate laughed.

"They're just like everybody else. They see a long black limousine and they lose their heads altogether."

"Yeah," said Sport. "They didn't even ask us."

"Listen," said Mr. Rocque. "About this arm now. Let's take you over to Doctor Phyth and get you looked at."

"They get you, Sport?" said Seymour. "I saw

that old lady pulling you. Wonder you got an arm at all."

"Boys," said Mr. Rocque. They all looked at him. "I hope it never comes to this, but I might need your help. You might have to testify to what happened today."

"Sure!" said Seymour. Harry and Chi-chi said nothing. Mr. Rocque looked at them.

"Harry was the one saw them get me," said Sport.

"Then you will be very valuable," said Mr. Rocque.

"And Chi-chi got me out the hotel," said Sport.

"You'll be the star witness," said Mr. Rocque.

"Geez, what'll I wear?" said Harry.

"Whew," said Seymour. "Get him. I bet he prays to Robert Hall."

"I've got to get on the phone again, call Sam, my lawyer," said Mr. Rocque. He stood up, looking tired. "One thing, she's blown her case now, he says, with this kidnapping gavotte. Wait'll this hits the papers tomorrow morning. She couldn't get the custody of a raccoon."

"Yeah?" said Sport.

"You gonna lose the money?" asked Harry.

"No," said Mr. Rocque. "She will."

"Hooray!" yelled Seymour.

The phone rang. Mr. Rocque sprinted to it, picked it up, shouted, "Hello!" then listened a long time, murmuring things like "Yeah?" and "No kidding?" They all stood watching him.

He turned to them finally and yelled. "It's Sam. He says she's given up."

"Hooray!" yelled Seymour.

"She's giving up any claim at all," shouted Mr. Rocque.

"Hooray!" shouted Seymour and Sport.

"She doesn't want the publicity. She's leaving for Europe tonight!" said Mr. Rocque.

"Hooray!" shouted Seymour and Sport and Harry.

"Sam says she's already left for the airport!" said Mr. Rocque.

"Hooray!" yelled Seymour and Sport and Harry and Chi-chi and Kate.

"Carrie has been in a faint all day!" said Mr. Rocque, giggling.

"Hooray!" yelled everybody.

Kate said, "Oh, Sport," and hugged him.

"Hey, man, you're rich too!" said Harry.

"Ech, who needs it?" said Sport.

"Clothes, man, you can buy clothes!" said Harry wildly. "What are you, crazy?" Harry looked terribly agitated, as though someone were stealing all his clothes.

"Geez," said Seymour, "another tie."

"You could go to college," said Chi-chi quietly.

"You could get a Cadillac," said Seymour.

"Naw, a Rolls," said Harry disdainfully.

"And kidnap little boys for money," said Sport sourly.

"Hey!" said Harry. "You could give all the money to LEWD."

The boys grinned.

"What's that?" said Kate.

"Uh . . ." said Harry.

"Nothing," said Sport. "Something for kids."